Strong hands held her steady against the hard warmth of his naked body

"Actions speak louder than words, darling, and what your lips deny, your body aches for."

Scarlet-faced, she tried to push him away. "No."

"Not fifteen minutes ago you were begging me to love you. Now I think you might appreciate and begin to feel some of the anguish my brother felt when you refused his love," Benedict said gloatingly, and, lifting her up as though she weighed no more than a feather, he dropped her back down on the bed.

JACQUELINE BAIRD began writing as a hobby when her family objected to the smell of her oil painting! She immediately became hooked on the romance genre. Jacqueline loves traveling and worked her way around the world from Europe to the Americas and Australia, returning to marry her teenage sweetheart. The couple now live in Ponteland, Northumbria, with their two teenage sons. She enjoys playing badminton, and spends most weekends with husband Jim, sailing on the Derwent Reservoir.

Books by Jacqueline Baird

JACQUELINE BAIRD

Guilty Passion

Harlequin Books

TORONTO • NEW YORK • LONDON
AMSTERDAM • PARIS • SYDNEY • HAMBURG
STOCKHOLM • ATHENS • TOKYO • MILAN
MADRID • WARSAW • BUDAPEST • AUCKLAND

ISBN 0-373-11627-6

GUILTY PASSION

CHAPTER ONE

REBECCA cast a look around the lecture theatre, before taking her seat in the front row, beside her boss. It was almost full. 'You were right, Rupert, it does seem to be popular,' she conceded, smiling at the man sitting next to her.

'Aren't I always?' he grinned. 'Shh. Here he comes.'

She returned his grin. Rebecca had come to the anthropological lecture only because Rupert had insisted. Rupert and his wife Mary had been students together with Benedict Maxwell, tonight's speaker.

'Good evening, ladies and gentlemen, I am flattered by your presence here tonight and I trust my experiences and discoveries of the past several years will live up to your expectations. If I become too boring you have my permission to walk out.'

Boring! The sound of his voice alone was mesmerising. Rebecca's head shot up, her startled glance colliding with dark, golden-flecked eyes that held her gaze for an instant before flicking to her companion. The man possessed a sexual magnetism that ignited a totally unexpected feminine response deep inside her. The breath caught in her throat, her heart missed a beat; nothing like this had ever happened to her before. Her large violet eyes widened to their fullest extent, her lips parted in an astonished moue. She knew him. It was insane—she had never met the man before—but deep down in some secret part of her she recognised him. Everything about him seemed so familiar...

5

Common sense told her she was being ridiculous but never in her life had she reacted so physically to a man. A slow heat suffused her body, she shook her small head in an instinctive gesture of denial, but it was futile as she felt herself being drawn under the spell of the man's vibrant personality.

He held centre stage with an ease and command few men possessed. He was tall, probably about six feet, superbly built with wide shoulders and a broad chest, tapering to a neat waist and long muscular legs; not an ounce of flab marred his large frame—the physique beneath the tweed jacket and expensive trousers was that of a man in peak condition.

Rebecca listened, entranced, to his tale of adventure and hardship. Six years ago he had set off on an expedition through the Amazon jungle; twelve months later he was reported dead by his guide and porters. They had seen him swept down the river and over a waterfall; no man could have survived the accident. But miraculously he had returned to civilisation a year ago, after having spent four years living and studying a hitherto unknown tribe of Indians. His book on his exploits was to be published the following week, and Rebecca had no doubt it would capture the imagination of a much larger public than the usual anthropological studies.

If he wrote half as well as he told a story, there could be no doubt about it, she thought, captivated, and hanging on to his every word. He painted pictures with his voice, his expressive features, a mere twist of his sensuous lips highlighting a point he wanted to make.

Little was known of him, but now he had appeared on the academic scene and shaken it to the core. Some of the more conservative anthropologists had a hard time hiding their jealousy. But Benedict Maxwell, ignoring the criticism, was embarking on a round of public lectures to keep the plight of the South American Indians and the devastation of the rain forests alive in the eyes of the world, and hopefully the world leaders would be forced to find a solution to the ever-increasing problem.

Rebecca was a hundred per cent in favour of his ideals, but, even if she had not been, just watching him would have convinced her.

His hair was black and rather long, a few wayward curls curving over the collar of his jacket. Taking his features one by one, he was not strictly handsome. His broad forehead, and black, rather bushy eyebrows, gave his face a rather sinister slant, along with a rather large crooked nose, and a hard square jaw. The overall impression was one of power and determination. But his eyes were truly beautiful...

Rebecca had never known two hours pass so quickly, and she was on her feet and applauding loudly when he finally concluded his lecture. For a second his golden-brown eyes rested on her and fancifully she was reminded of some large jungle hunting cat, but then a frown marred his rugged face and the moment was gone.

She turned excitedly to Rupert. 'He was brilliant, absolutely brilliant.'

Rupert laughed. He was a big rumpled-looking man with a shaggy mane of grey hair that reinforced the impression. When her father was ill Rupert had employed her as his research assistant. Then, when her Dad had died some months ago and she had sold the family home, she had become Rupert and Mary's lodger.

He reached out and slung a casual arm around her slender shoulders. 'You too.' He shook his large head. 'I don't know... first Mary went into raptures when she heard Ben was coming, and now it looks as if you're smitten as well.'

Rebecca laughed, and, tossing her head in a vain attempt to disperse the giddy feeling Benedict Maxwell had aroused in her, she teased, 'Shame on you, Rupert, you know Mary has eyes for no one but you, and of course tiny Jonathan.'

'Yes.' A satisfied smile creased Rupert's face, and Rebecca knew why. His wife had given birth to a baby boy a week ago, their first child after ten years of marriage. Mother and child had returned home only yesterday. 'Look, would you mind going to the party at the Chancellor's rooms and making my excuses? I'll call in later. First, I want to check on Mary.'

'Of course, Rupert. Give them my love,' she smiled.

Still smiling, Rebecca walked across the quadrangle and made her way to the administration block. She stopped outside the Chancellor's door then turned quickly and headed for the ladies' toilet. The nervous flutter in her stomach she put down to indigestion, but in her heart she knew she was only lying to herself—the thought of meeting Benedict Maxwell face to face filled her with a trembling excitement she had never experienced before. Pull yourself together, my girl, she told herself, and, placing her handbag on the washbasin, she studied her reflection in the mirror above.

Was that flushed, sparkling-eyed girl really her? She was behaving like a fool. Determinedly she splashed cool water on her face and dabbed it dry, and, opening her bag, she carefully repaired her make-up—what little there was of it. A touch more mascara on her long, thick lashes, a fresh covering of pink gloss to her full lips, and with a sigh she viewed the result.

It was hopeless. She was educated, intelligent and good at her job as a researcher for Professor Rupert Bart, a senior lecturer in law—she was a match for any man. Unfortunately, at five feet tall, with large pansy eyes, and long black hair that, although pinned up in a chignon, had a nasty tendency to curl, plus a shape that was a little too curvaceous, she looked like a seventeen-year-old Lolita! She winced at the thought, an ugly memory shadowing her eyes.

She sighed; even the severely cut straight blue silk shift could not disguise the fullness of her breasts, the feminine curve of her hips. The great man would never notice her. Even if he did, he would never take her seriously on sight. No man ever had...

Rebecca stood in one corner of the lavishly furnished room and listened to the conversations going on around her with half an ear, intensely aware of the man who held court in the middle of the room, surrounded by some of the best brains in Oxford. She had given Rupert's apologies to the Chancellor, and could not help noticing that the man's secretary, Fiona Grieves, a tall redhead, had latched on to the guest of honour and was clinging to his arm like a limpet.

Chancellor Foster had casually introduced Rebecca to Benedict Maxwell, and as she had stood tongue-tied he had murmured a polite response, and with a purely social smile that had not reached his eyes—in fact he had looked almost disapproving—he had continued his conversation with Fiona. Rebecca, hurt at his offhand manner, quietly slipped into the background, but from her relative seclusion she feasted her eyes on the man of her dreams.

'Rebecca, it is not like you to be hiding in a corner—come and let me introduce you to Benedict.'

She jumped at the sound of Rupert's voice and, placing her glass on the window-sill beside her, she reluctantly walked the few paces to where he was standing with Benedict, Fiona and the Chancellor. She felt a complete fool. She opened her mouth to say they had already been introduced, but Rupert cut in.

Flinging his arm around her shoulder and drawing her into the little circle, he said, 'This is Rebecca, my personal assistant. You remember old Bruiser, Ben? Well,

this is his daughter, and just as clever as the old man
was.'

'Bruiser? Rupert!' she admonished lightly, while
wishing the ground would open and swallow her up. Why
Benedict Maxwell affected her so strangely, she had no
idea, and she wasn't sure she liked the feeling.

Rupert laughed. 'Sorry, pet, it was our nickname for
him. Blacket-Green equals Bruiser!'

She managed to smile, until Benedict Maxwell turned
and, freeing his arm from Fiona, fixed his brilliant
leonine eyes on Rebecca.

'The late Professor Blacket-Green's daughter?'
Surprise and some other emotion she did not recognise
coloured his voice as he questioned her.

'You knew my father?' she asked quietly.

'I attended a few of his lectures. He died recently, I
believe.' His hooded lids half closed, masking his dark
eyes as he added, 'My condolences. I know what it feels
like to lose someone you love.'

She recognised the sympathy in his deep, melodious
tone, and her earlier apprehension vanished; she was
completely captivated, and it showed as she smiled up
at his ruggedly attractive face.

'Thank you.'

His dark gaze slid over her from head to toe, and there
was no mistaking the masculine interest in his scrutiny.
She did not question why he had barely noticed her when
they were first introduced, but basked in his obvious male
appreciation.

The rest of the evening passed in a dream for Rebecca.
Benedict insisted on getting her a glass of champagne,
and keeping her by his side, a hand placed casually on
her slender shoulders. The conversation was lively and
informative, and eventually light-hearted as Rupert insisted on showing everyone a photograph of his new son.

'Where is Mary tonight?' Benedict queried.

Whereupon Rupert regaled Benedict with all the technical details of the birth with obvious pride, ending on a joking note, 'But Mary reckons the boy is too young to be deprived of his food source just yet. So my personal, live-in assistant here, who got a double first last year—quite some achievement for such a tich——' he patted Rebecca on the head, much to her fury '—was detailed to look after me, to keep my spirits up. Along with this.' And, lifting a half-full glass of whisky to his lips, he drained it.

'You live with Rupert?' The censorious tone of Benedict's voice was obvious.

'No... Well, yes.' She stumbled over her words in her haste to explain. Did all women feel like this, she wondered, when they met the man of their dreams? She was desperate that this man should have a good opinion of her. 'I mean, I'm lodging with Mary and Rupert. I sold my father's house, and I intend to buy a small apartment, when I decide where I want to live, but in the meantime Mary asked me to stay and help with the baby and everything...' She was babbling, and her voice tailed off as her violet eyes were trapped and held by brilliant gold.

He smiled down into her bemused face. 'I understand, Rebecca.'

She was sure he did; she felt a sensuous longing to reach out and trace the full line of his lips, to feel them against her own. 'Thank you,' she murmured, not really sure what she was thanking him for, or where her erotic fantasies were coming from.

Benedict lifted his hand and gently tilted her chin with one finger. 'It's rather crowded here, and I would very much like to get to know you better, Miss Blacket-Green,' he drawled softly and before she knew what was happening she found herself backed into the corner of the large bay window.

'So, Rebecca, tell me—what does a young girl who hardly looks old enough to have left school intend doing with a first from Oxford? Surely not work as a researcher for old Rupert all your life?' One dark eyebrow rose enquiringly.

To Rebecca's astonishment she found herself telling him all her hopes for the future. 'I had intended to go to Nottingham for a year and get my postgraduate Certificate of Education, and then into teaching. But with Father ill I stayed at home and looked after him until his death six months ago.'

She did not regret it. Instead it had allowed her to accept the fact of his death that much more easily.

'So what are you going to do now?' Benedict asked quietly.

'Well, in September I'm going to complete my education, albeit a year late. Eventually I hope to teach high school history and French.'

'Teaching...not very ambitious for a girl with your——' he drawled the word '—qualificatons.' His lingering glance added a sensuous message—he was not just referring to her academic achievements—while the hand on her shoulder slid around the back of her neck.

She trembled at the warmth of his touch, and went pink with embarrassment, and a flash of anger. It was one of her pet hates when people derided the teaching profession, and somehow she had expected better of Benedict.

'Your attitude surprises me, Mr Maxwell, considering your education.' She knew from Rupert that Benedict had a first in maths as well as a B.A. and a D.Phil. 'I hate the kind of attitude, which seems to be prevalent in our country, that people only go into teaching for lack of any real ambition.' She tilted her head at his urging, and was stung by the gentle amusement infusing the darkness of his rugged features. 'I'm sorry if my opinions amuse you. But you are not the first person to suggest I should take up a more lucrative career. The City, or business. Do you know I was even approached by Chase Manhattan of New York?' She came to an abrupt halt, as Benedict laughed out loud.

'Well, well, you are quite a surprise, Rebecca; you look so cool and controlled when really you're quite a little firecracker.'

She flushed bright red; his hand still curved her slender neck and suddenly she lost all her anger, as the caress of his strong fingers sent shivers of awareness tingling down her spine. 'I'm sorry, I'm afraid I talk too much. With all you've seen and done, my aspirations must seem very boring,' she managed, wondering why her voice sound so husky.

'Not at all, Rebecca, and I apologise if my earlier comment offended you. It wasn't meant to. I think teaching is a very laudable profession, and, as for finding you boring, you couldn't be more wrong. Everything about you intrigues me.'

She looked at him uncertainly; he sounded sincere. The golden-brown eyes darkened, an unmistakable message in their depths as they lingered on her flushed, upturned face then very deliberately dropped lower to where her full breasts thrust taut against the soft silk of her dress. Her blush deepened and she was more flustered than she had ever been in her life. She raised her hand to her throat in an unconscious attempt to conceal the pulse that beat heavily under her skin.

'You will make a wonderful teacher, though I think you may have problems with the young men.'

'Because I'm small?' she answered resignedly. He had disappointed her. Rupert was always teasing her with that fact.

'No, your size is perfect, but you look so young, all the male students are bound to fall in love with you.'

'I'm twenty-two,' she bristled.

Benedict slowly trailed long fingers back around to her shoulder, and gently squeezed. 'I didn't mean to offend you, Rebecca, but at thirty-four everyone in their twenties appears young to me.' He pulled her tight against his side. 'But not too young... Am I forgiven?' he murmured throatily.

She could not disguise the tremor of awareness that the contact with his hard body aroused in her. Her breast brushed lightly against the fine wool of his jacket and the tightening of her nipples made her catch her breath. Her glance lifted to his face, her eyes wide and wondering, she lifted her hand and placed it on his chest; she could feel the slow, steady thump of his heart beneath her fingertips, but she was unaware of the total intimacy of her gesture, and in that moment she would have forgiven the man murder.

'Yes, oh, yes,' she murmured. One part of her mind was answering his question while another, more primitive part was accepting the vibrant masculine demand in his darkening gaze.

Benedict captured the small hand that lay on his chest, turned it palm-up and, raising it to his lips, planted a soft kiss in the middle of her palm. 'I think we understand each other, you and I...'

She was captivated, completely enthralled, her violet eyes darkened to deep purple, her lips parted seductively. She felt as though she was drowning in the dark golden depths of his eyes.

'Now is not the time or the place, Rebecca. Dinner tomorrow night. I'll call for you at seven.'

She loved the sound of her name rolling huskily off his tongue. 'Yes,' she whispered, her breathing erratic, as he lowered his dark head and planted another kiss on her softly parted lips.

'Duty calls, I have to circulate.'

Rebecca's circulation had gone berserk at the touch of his lips on hers, the blood flowing through her veins like wildfire.

'Goodnight for now, little one, but don't forget me.' He smiled down into her delicate flushed face. 'Until tomorrow.' His hand dropped from her shoulder, he tapped her chin with one long finger. 'And don't worry, Rebecca, I like my ladies chin-high.' He grinned and winked as he walked away.

How long she stood with a silly grin on her face, she had no idea. It was only when she looked around her that she realised what a spectacle they must have made. She could see the knowing smiles on quite a few female faces, but she didn't care. She had met Benedict for the first time tonight, but already she was in love with him. She knew it with absolute certainty.

'Well, my pet, old Ben has certainly knocked you for six, if your soppy expression is anything to go by.' Rupert's voice brought her back to reality with a jolt.

'Is it so obvious?' she asked quietly, tearing her gaze away from where Benedict stood, once again surrounded by people, to focus on her boss.

'I'm afraid so, little one. But a word of warning. Benedict is not the sort of man you should cut your milk-teeth on.'

'I'm not a baby, I do know about sex.' She grinned at Rupert. 'Benedict is taking me to dinner tomorrow night.' Just saying the words out loud thrilled her to the core.

'Ah-ah. Before you do anything foolish, girl, I suggest you have a chat with Mary. She knows Ben better than me. They were good friends as students. He is a very complex man, and, to be brutally frank, I think a bit out of your league.'

'Thanks, friend,' she responded drily. 'You're a great confidence-booster.' She watched as Rupert ran a huge hand through his untidy mass of grey hair, and almost felt sorry for him, he looked so perplexed.

'Oh, hell, Becky, you know what I mean. Just be careful—and now let's get out of here.' He watched her scan the room for the man they had been discussing and when she found him, even Rupert could see that the look that passed between Rebecca and Benedict would have lit coals.

She responded to Benedict's rueful shrug of broad shoulders, and a softly mouthed, 'Tomorrow,' with a brilliant smile and a very determined nod of her lovely head.

Rebecca, with one last lingering glance at Benedict, allowed Rupert to lead her out of the overcrowded room, and down to the quadrangle. Arm in arm, they strolled through the streets of Oxford. Rebecca thought the town had never looked more beautiful. Early June, and the students had almost finished their exams. The old place vibrated with young voices filled with exultation and relief.

The mellowed stone of the great colleges gleamed faintly silver in the fading light, and Rebecca's heart sang with unaccustomed joy. She walked on air for the ten minutes it took to reach the large brown stone terrace that was her temporary home.

Sitting across the table from Mary in the kitchen, her small hands curved around a cup of cocoa, she tried to remain cool in the face of Mary's demand to know what Maxwell's lecture had been like.

'OK, Rebecca,' Mary exclaimed. The older woman drained her cocoa-cup, and replaced it on the table, before fixing Rebecca with gimlet blue eyes. 'Why don't you forget the high ideals to save the world and tell me what really happened?'

Rebecca sat up straight in the chair, a wry smile curving her full lips; was she really so transparent? Even Mary, who was ordinarily completely engrossed in her new role as mother, noticed her emotional upheaval.

'Benedict Maxwell has happened,' she said bluntly—prevarication was not her style.

'Ah! So it's Ben who has turned you from a beautiful woman into a radiant one. I should have guessed. He always did have a disastrous effect on the female of the species, even as a student.'

'I wish I had known him then,' Rebecca mused; the thought of Benedict as a child and young man, all the years he had lived before she had met him, filled her with mixed emotions. Was it jealousy? No, surely not. Just greed; she had an avid desire to know every little thing about the man who had so instantly captured her heart.

'Tell me about him, Mary.' She looked at her companion, and flinched as a horrible thought struck her. Had Mary been one of his women? She was a very pretty lady, tall with brown hair and laughing blue eyes, and the personality to match. Benedict might have been her lover...

'No, he wasn't my boyfriend,' Mary chuckled, accurately reading Rebecca's thoughts. 'But we all went around in the same group. As for telling you about him, I don't know what to say. Apart from exchanging Christmas cards for a few years I've never seen him in the flesh since we left college. He must have changed quite a lot, in the intervening years, from the shy young man I knew.'

'Shy?' Rebecca exclaimed; somehow that was not a trait she would ever have associated with Benedict.

'Yes. Well, perhaps shy is not the right word. Reserved maybe.' A reminiscent smile curved Mary's wide mouth. 'Most of the time, that is, but I remember one occasion, the end of our second-year exams. We were all at a party, and I reckon it was the first and only time Ben got drunk.

He and I talked all night. I know his father died when he was ten, and within months his mother had married again, Ben was shunted off to boarding school and by the time he was twelve he had a baby brother.'

Rebecca's heart ached for the young boy losing his father and stuck away in a boarding school. Her own mother had died when she was nine, and she could appreciate the loneliness Benedict must have suffered.

Mary continued, 'He was a very complex young man. I know he explained his mother's quick remarriage by saying she was a timid woman who needed the support of a man. I got the impression he felt a shade guilty because he was too young to give her what she needed.' Mary sighed. 'The naïve intensity of youth! The woman probably wanted a man in her bed... Anyway, apart from that one evening, Benedict never discussed his personal life again. There's not much else I can tell you, except I liked him.'

'You've told me quite a lot already. I know you probably think I've flipped my lid, but just hearing you talk about him fills me with pleasure.' Rebecca grinned, her eyes sparkling with mischief. 'I'm seeing him tomorrow night and will carry out my own investigation—I can hardly wait.'

'I can see it's only his brilliant mind you are interested in, nothing so crass as his gorgeous body,' Mary teased, and they both burst out laughing.

When their laughter stopped, Mary reached across the table and took Rebecca's hand in hers. 'Don't get me wrong, I know you're a very capable lady, but when it comes to affairs of the heart you don't have much experience. Benedict is a lot older than you, and I don't want to see you get hurt. Be very sure it's not just a case of hero worship, before you do anything stupid.'

Rebecca squeezed Mary's fingers, and, with naïve honesty, responded, 'I have never felt like this about a man before. I just know deep down he's the one for me, and if I get hurt, so be it.'

Later, much later, she was to realise the bitter truth of her words.

CHAPTER TWO

REBECCA looked at the jumble of clothes covering her bed, and sighed. Benedict would be here in half an hour, and here she was, still standing virtually naked except for tiny white lace briefs, trying to decide what to wear.

It was her own fault, she thought, a snort of self-disgust escaping her. If she had not spent the best part of the Saturday afternoon washing her hair, doing her nails and wallowing in the bath for hours, reliving in her mind her meeting with Benedict, and fantasising about the evening ahead, she might have had the sense to go out and buy something to wear. Now, she was all made-up—well, made-up for her. A moisturiser was all she needed and a slight touch of mascara on her long lashes, but she was stuck with the rather sparse wardrobe she had acquired as a student, and added to only briefly in the past year.

Finally, she opted for the last garment in her wardrobe. Still in its plastic cover was the rose-coloured silk suit she had bought only days earlier, in anticipation of baby Jonathan's christening. What the hell? she told herself. I can buy something else. And carefully removed it.

The pencil-slim skirt hugged her hips and ended just on her knee. The matching camisole with shoe-string straps prevented her wearing a bra, but one quick glance and modesty had her grabbing the fitted silk short-sleeved jacket and slipping it on. Double-breasted, it fastened with two buttons neatly at her trim waist. She surveyed the whole ensemble, pleased with the result. As long as she kept the jacket on she'd be fine. Quickly she applied the new matching soft pink lip-gloss to her full lips.

She pivoted in front of the cheval-glass, and wished, for the hundredth time, that she were taller, before slipping her feet into moderate-heeled navy sandals. It wouldn't be so bad if she could wear four-inch heels, but the one time she had tried she sprained her ankle.

Still, Benedict had said he liked his ladies chin-high, she consoled herself. She viewed her hair with some misgivings. She had swept it up at each side and held it with two gilt combs, allowing the long black tresses to fall in shining waves down her back. She should have pinned it all up; a more sophisticated image might have helped her look older. She reached for the comb...

The ringing of the doorbell set her heart pounding. Too late now... And, grabbing her lipstick, she shoved it in a small navy clutch-bag, and dashed out of the room.

Careful, she told herself and forced her feet to slow down. She heard the sound of Mary's voice and laughter and the deeper, more earthy tone of Benedict, as they renewed their acquaintance.

She was halfway down the stairs when she caught sight of Benedict; her breath caught in her throat and she almost fell down the last few steps.

He moved quickly across the hall and caught her arm. 'Steady, Rebecca.'

She had the sinking feeling she would never be steady in this man's company in a million years, and for the first time since meeting him the force of her feelings for him scared her.

Tonight he was dressed in an immaculate silver-grey suit, his silk shirt a soft blue. A grey and blue striped tie drew her attention to his strong, tanned throat. Slowly she raised her head, as his eyes roamed hotly over her body and face. 'Hello, Benedict,' was all she could manage, unable to tear her eyes from his.

'You look absolutely beautiful, Rebecca. You must
always wear your hair loose for me.' And, raising his
other hand, he slid his fingers through the thickness of
her hair, pulling a few strands over her shoulder, his
long fingers tracing the length down over the soft swell
of her breast in an erotic gesture that sent shock waves
of pleasure arcing through her body...

'I can see I'm *de trop* here. Have a good time,
children.' Mary's voice broke the spell that bound them.
'And don't keep her out all night,' she added to Benedict.

'We will, Mary, and don't worry; unlike her other men
friends, I will bring her back safely.'

What other men friends? Rebecca thought, not sure
how to take the obvious cynicism in his tone. But, when
Benedict encircled her slender waist with one arm to
escort her from the house to the waiting car, his touch
knocked every sensible thought from her head. She slid
into the passenger-seat, and, fighting down the nervous
tension that engulfed her, she sank back against the soft
leather upholstery. In a way his car surprised her, when
she came to her senses enough to notice it was a top-of-
the-range Mercedes. Academics in England were not
particularly well paid.

'Alone at last.' Benedict grinned as he slid in behind
the driving-wheel and started the car. 'I thought my days
of courting in a car were long over, but I have a horrible
suspicion that, as long as you live with Rupert and Mary,
that will be my fate.' He cast her a sidelong glance, his
golden-brown eyes sparkling merrily. 'Unless I can persuade you to move in with me,' he teased.

'I might if I knew where you lived,' Rebecca said
lightly; she knew he was only flirting but she could not
help her pulse racing at the thought of sharing a home,
a bed, with this gorgeous man by her side.

'I have a hut in the Amazonian rain forest or a place
in London. Which would you prefer?'

She chuckled. 'Guess.'

Benedict's light-hearted banter set the tone for the rest of the evening. They drove out of Oxford to a small roadside inn that looked like something from a picture-postcard—thatch-roofed and old oak beams.

Over a quite simple meal of steak and salad followed by cheese and biscuits Rebecca finally relaxed. The bottle of fine Bordeaux wine helped. It was amazing how much they had in common, she thought wonderingly, as the conversation moved from theatre, to music, to politics, and, at Rebecca's insistence, to Benedict's time in the jungle. He made her laugh with his anecdotes but she knew it had not been easy for him. He had been badly injured when the Indians found him, and it had taken over a year before he had recovered his health and then another three before making his seemingly miraculous return to civilisation.

'I am an honorary member of the tribe, and have my own hut; perhaps I can tempt you to share it with me?' he grinned.

'Surely the chief gave you his daughter? Isn't that what usually happens?' she prompted teasingly.

'The offer was made. Unfortunately all the unmarried girls were barely thirteen and somehow I couldn't bring myself to have sex with a child. I adopted a celibate life-style.' His gaze darkened perceptibly and she gasped at the expression in his eyes. 'But, since meeting you, that's about to change. You don't strike me as the sort of woman to deny herself the pleasures of the flesh,' he decided sensuously.

'Coffee, sir.' The waiter broke the tension that arced between them.

Rebecca did not know whether to be flattered or insulted by his comment, and to hide her disquiet she blurted the first thing that came into her head. 'The poor man probably thinks you're some kind of paedophile,' she gibed. 'Or mad, Benedict.'

His gaze was fixed on her beautiful face, and slowly he reached across the table and took her small hand in his much larger one, his thumb gently stroking the palm of her hand. 'I am mad—mad about you. I love to hear you say my name in that breathless tone.' He lifted her hand and pressed a kiss on the pulse that beat rapidly in her wrist. She shivered and would have pulled her hand free, suddenly embarrassed—there were other people around. 'No, Rebecca, don't back off now; your honesty was one of the first things I noticed about you.' He tightened his grip. 'You know what's happening be-tween us, don't you?' he demanded hardly.

Rebecca swallowed the lump that formed in her throat, almost choked by her own emotions. It was not just her, her heart sang. He felt it too, this familiarity, this secret knowledge of each other. She tried to tell herself it was too quick—love at first sight was a myth—but still she murmured softly, 'Yes, oh, yes.' Her violet eyes, wide and full of longing, searched his rugged features, and the desire she saw in his told her all she needed to know.

'If you keep looking at me like that, Rebecca, I'm going to drag you out of here by that magnificent hair and I doubt if we'll make it past the car park.'

She flushed bright red and hastily looked down at the table. 'I'm sorry, it's... I don't know.' And, bravely raising her head, she said, 'I've never felt this way before.' She was incapable of dissembling.

'I want to believe that, Rebecca. God, how I want to believe that.' For a second she imagined she saw shock in his eyes but she must have been mistaken, as he slowly shook his dark head. 'But an intelligent, beautiful woman like you must have had many admirers. Is there anyone now I should know about?'

'No, Benedict, not now, not ever, only you.'

Abruptly he dropped her hand and sat back in his chair, his eyes narrowing speculatively. 'I find that hard to believe but I'll take your word for it.' He paused. 'For the moment.'

Rebecca did not understand what he meant, but before she could ask he had beckoned the waiter. 'Let's get out of here; suddenly the place seems too crowded.' Passing a bundle of notes to the waiter, he stood up, and held out a hand to Rebecca.

Back once more in the car, Benedict turned towards her, sliding one long arm around her slender shoulders, then he lowered his dark head and she knew he was going to kiss her. 'I want you,' he murmured against her lips, before covering her mouth with his own.

She trembled in his arms, the heat of his taut body engulfing her, the pressure of his mouth on hers almost painful in its intensity, as he kissed her hard and long. The force of his passion at first surprised then swamped her. She responded with all the fervour of a young heart awakening to love. When his hand slid inside her jacket and then eased down her camisole, she tensed, wary at the intimacy, but as his hand cupped her breast, his thumb teasing the hardening peak, an intoxication she had never dreamed of flooded through her slender body.

'Benedict,' she whimpered as his head dropped lower and his mouth covered the madly beating pulse in her throat, while his hand continued to caress her burgeoning breast.

She was aflame with a need, a hunger, she could not control, did not want to. The blood pulsed through her veins like wildfire. She raised her arms around his shoulders, her small hand burrowed into the silky strands of his black hair, holding him to her. She felt no shame; surely this was what she was born for...

Benedict groaned and slowly raised his head; carefully he eased her away from him and, with hands that shook, he straightened her clothing. 'God, Rebecca, I almost took you in the car park after all. You have a devastating effect on me, little one.'

'I'm glad,' she whispered fiercely, still aching for his caress, his kisses. 'I think I'm falling in love with you, and it would be terrible if it was all one-sided.' She tried to laugh, knowing she had told him more than she should.

Benedict cupped her small face between his palms. His golden-brown eyes burned into hers. 'It's no joke, Rebecca. I feel the same as you do, but here is not the place to show you.' He pressed a swift kiss on her swollen lips, before he let her go and turned to face the front. 'I'd better get you home before Rupert sends out a search party. But make no mistake, Rebecca, this is just the beginning for you and me. I promise.'

They drove back to Oxford in a companionable silence. Benedict accepted her invitation for coffee, but to her chagrin Rupert joined them. Still, she consoled herself, Benedict had said it was just the beginning and she believed him. Later, when he left, she walked to his car with him. Surely he would ask to see her again; he must... she thought furiously, and she had no idea how expressive her small face was as she murmured, 'Goodnight, Benedict,' knowing she could delay him no longer.

'If you keep looking at me like that, Rebecca, I will be tempted to bundle you in the car, and take you back to London with me,' he teased.

'I wish you would,' she joked, half seriously.

He pulled her into his arms, and, bending his head, kissed her long and hard. 'I'm lecturing on Monday at UCL, but I will be in touch.'

By the following Wednesday Rebecca's sense of euphoria was fading fast. She had hardly been out of the house, but Benedict had not called. Finally, at Mary's urging, she agreed to go to the local historical society's monthly meeting. She sat through the talk and film show, only half aware of what was going on, but worse, when she returned home, Mary met her with a wry smile. Benedict had called.

'Oh, no. I knew I should have stayed in.'

'Rubbish, girl. He said to tell you he'd called and...'

'And what?' Rebecca demanded, unable to stand the suspense.

'I've invited him to stay the weekend. He will be arriving Saturday, but he'll call tomorrow night to confirm when.'

Rebecca flung herself on Mary. 'You darling.'

On Thursday night Rebecca waited by the phone. When it finally rang she was filled with an unaccountable nervousness.

'The Bart residence,' she answered, hoping, after a few false alarms, that this call would be Benedict.

'Rebecca. I'm honoured, I've finally caught you in. What happened? Have you worn out the young beaux of Oxford?' he drawled mockingly.

'Benedict,' she said, hurt he could imagine she would dream of going out with anyone else. For a horrifying moment the thought crossed her mind; perhaps Benedict had heard about her brief twenty-four hours of notoriety years ago. No, he couldn't possibly—he had not even been in the country at the time. Anyway, she could explain the unfortunate episode. Benedict would understand, but not yet. She wanted nothing to mar her new-found love. Hastily she began explaining the reason for her absence the night before, while telling herself she was worrying unnecessarily.

'It's all right, Rebecca, I believe you, but to get down to business. I'll be with you at about three on Saturday afternoon. OK?'

'Oh, yes!' she breathed happily, and dismissed the odd feeling that he did not believe her as so much nonsense.

* * *

June gave way to July and Rebecca would have given way to Benedict if he had asked her... But he hadn't.

She stood looking out of the window of the living-room, waiting for him to arrive. She spoke to him frequently on the telephone and for the past three weekends he had returned to Oxford and stayed with her, and Mary, Rupert and baby Jonathan... Perhaps that was the problem.

A secret smile curved her full lips, but not any more... This weekend she had the house to herself. Rupert had taken the family to his parents in Devon to show off the new grandson.

Rebecca could barely control her excitement. She loved Benedict and she was almost sure he loved her. They'd shared intimate dinners, gone to concerts, spent one glorious Sunday sailing up the river, and the passionate kisses they exchanged each time he arrived and departed left her weak at the knees and longing for more.

She smoothed her damp palms over her slim hips. They would be alone, completely alone, for two whole days... Her heartbeat raced at the thought, then leapt as she saw his car draw up at the door. She ran through the hall, opened the door, and flung herself into his arms.

'Now, that is what I call a welcome!' Benedict growled, before lowering his dark head and kissing her firmly on the mouth.

He ended the kiss far too soon for Rebecca, and as he eased her away from him his eyes narrowed in knowing amusement. 'What have I done to deserve this passionate welcome, little one?'

She searched his rugged face with hungry eyes, drinking in the sight of him. 'Nothing,' she murmured in response, 'but I've missed you.'

'I know the feeling,' he said quietly. 'But how about letting me get in the door? Rupert, man of letters that he is, will not appreciate a couple making love on his doorstep,' he drawled mockingly.

'He won't know.' She couldn't wait to tell him. 'We have the house to ourselves; they've gone to his parents for the weekend.' She grinned broadly and, grabbing Benedict's arm, led him into the hall. She closed the door behind her and turned towards him. 'Now I've caught you,' she teased, and, standing on tiptoe, flung her arms around his neck.

'Is that what you want?' His large tanned hands spanned her narrow waist, and lifted her so her face was on a level with his. 'To catch me? Or is this more to your liking?' And, swinging her high over his broad shoulders in a fireman's lift, he strode through the open door into the living-room.

She screamed, 'Benedict, put me down!' With her head hanging down his back and his strong arms wrapped firmly round her thighs, she was powerless to break free. 'You'll drop me.'

'I wouldn't dream of it, my darling girl,' he declared with a chuckle, then she was falling in a helpless bundle on to the large shabby leather sofa.

She lay on her back, her legs splayed apart, her hair a tumbled mass of black silk falling around her face and over her shoulders. She had no idea how seductive she looked: her brief white shorts barely covered her hips, the knitted T-shirt she was wearing had ridden up and left a teasing glimpse of naked midriff. Laughing, she stared up at Benedict. 'I think you've spent too long with the natives, my man.' She chuckled, 'You Tarzan, me Jane,' her wide pansy eyes, lit with laughter, clashing with his.

His golden gaze glittered over the vivid flush in her cheeks, the unconsciously wanton posture of her lovely body. A hint of derision flashed in the darkening depths, as Benedict bent over her and with one hand stroked the hair from her face. 'Are you trying to pretend a tiny beauty like you has never been picked up by a man before?'

The smile left her face. She had the oddest impression he was not referring to being bodily lifted, but something else entirely. 'My father used to,' she responded quietly.

He was towering over her, his strong legs encased in form-fitting black jeans that revealed the musculature of his thighs, and more. Her blush deepened, and she hastily raised her eyes to his broad chest, the thick curling body hair visible where he had left the top three buttons of his checked shirt unfastened.

Rebecca swallowed hard, her pulse racing, suddenly aware of their complete privacy. She stirred uneasily on the sofa, and began to rise.

'No. Stay where you are,' Benedict commanded, and, placing a hand on the top of her thigh, he nudged her slightly as he lowered himself down beside her. 'What did you say earlier about our having the house to ourselves?' he husked throatily, and, placing one hand on the back of the sofa, with the other he gently traced the line of her mouth.

Her lips parted of their own volition and lazily she reached slender arms up around his neck. God, how she loved him! she thought, mesmerised by the dark gleam in his wonderful eyes. The tantalising male scent of him filled her nostrils, and she wanted nothing more in this life than to lose herself in the warmth, the strength of his virile male body.

With the pad of one long finger he gently rubbed the inside of her bottom lip, his piercing gaze holding her captive. 'I want you, Rebecca, and I think you want me.'

'Oh, Benedict. I do, I do.' She had no thought of denying him.

'Do you love me, Rebecca? Really love me?'

A stray beam of sunlight slanted across his darkly tanned face, touching his black hair with gold, like a halo around his proud head, and for a moment masking the expression in his eyes. He looked like a Greek god to Rebecca; how could she help but love him?

'I love you, Benedict, I feel as though I always have, and I know I always will,' she told him.

His head swooped down and his mouth found hers. She whimpered as his teeth nibbled her lips, teasing, then suddenly, as she arched against him, her fingers burrowing in the thick dark hair that curled the nape of his neck, he groaned, his strong arms wrapping her tightly to his hard frame, as he deepened the kiss, his tongue probing the hot, dark secrets of her mouth with a greedy passion.

Abruptly he broke the kiss, and straightened up; with one hand on the soft curve of her breast he held her down on the sofa. Rebecca smiled up at him dazedly, her eyes like twin stars in the perfect oval of her flushed face. The smile faded, as she surprised an arrested expression on his rugged face.

'You, my dear, are dynamite—a real firecracker—and if I don't get away from here soon I'm liable to do something we may both regret.'

'I won't regret anything, Benedict, I promise.' And she raised a small hand, and did what she had been aching to do for weeks: trailed her fingers down his strong throat, and inside his open shirt, stroking over a hard male nipple buried in soft, silky hair.

'Now, I wonder how many men you've said that to?' He grasped her wrist and pulled her hand free.

'None. Only you.' Was he jealous, she wondered, or was it something else? She wished he would not talk like that, as though he doubted her. She shivered . . . Someone walked over her grave . . .

'Sit up, make yourself decent, if that's possible.'

'I don't think I liked that crack,' she muttered, sitting up and decorously tugging her T-shirt down.

Benedict did not respond; instead he put his hand in his back pocket, and drew out a small jeweller's box. His eyes were half closed and his thick, curling lashes almost brushed his cheek as he studied the box in his hand. 'This is something that belongs to you, Rebecca. I think you should have it before we go any further.'

Rebecca's heart slammed against her chest, her hand trembled, as she reached out. She lifted moisture-filled eyes to Benedict's face but he avoided her look. This wonderful man, who had braved all sorts of hardship in the Amazon, was shy. His vulnerability touched her, and a great rush of love almost caused her pain.

He placed the small red box in her outstretched hand, and slowly she opened the lid. It was exquisite—a deep violet-red stone surrounded with tiny diamonds.

'It's beautiful, Benedict, and I'm the luckiest girl in the whole world. Put it on for me.' And, holding out her left hand, she trembled as he slid the small ring on her finger.

'You like it?' he asked, still avoiding her eyes.

'I love it, the same way I love you, Benedict.'

'That figures,' he laughed, but somehow the sound was harsh.

Poor man, he really is nervous, she thought and, pushing her way on to his knee, she curled up in his lap. She could sense the tension in him, and, wrapping one arm around his neck, she extended her other arm, her fingers splayed, the better to admire her engagement ring. 'I love rubies.' She sighed her contentment.

'It's a garnet,' he corrected her flatly.

'Whatever,' she whispered; at last confident of his love, she planted a soft kiss on the strong brown column of his throat. 'I'll treasure it all our married life,' she mouthed against his satin-smooth skin.

Benedict murmured, 'I'm sure you will.' But she never heard the sarcasm in his voice as, tilting her chin with one long finger, he kissed her lightly on the lips. 'I'm sorry, Rebecca, but I can't stop. I only called down today to give you the ring. I have to go straight back to London; I'm appearing on a television chat show this evening.'

His news dimmed the happiness in her eyes. 'But what about us? Our engagement day and you're going to leave me. At the very least we should have a drink to celebrate.' She couldn't hide her disappointment.

'No, sorry, I'm driving.' Benedict lifted her off his lap, plonked her back on the sofa, and stood up.

'But we have tons to discuss, like a date for the wedding.' Just saying the words made Rebecca smile. So maybe they couldn't be together straight away, but they had all the time in the world, she realised. They would be man and wife. She was so happy; all her wildest dreams had come true.

'I will only be in England until the end of August, then I have to be in New York. Perhaps...' He hesitated.

With a radiant face she jumped up, not letting him finish the sentence. 'It only takes a couple of weeks to arrange a wedding and then I could come to America with you.'

Some expression in his eyes made her heart miss a beat.

'That's not a bad idea, but there are quite a few other considerations. I'll think about it and we can discuss it next week. There's no hurry, and I'm sure you're a great little organiser; whatever we decide, I have no doubt you will manage,' he drawled mockingly.

Rebecca smiled at his teasing, never registering the mockery. 'Whatever you say,' she sighed happily. She looked at the ring sparkling on her finger and all it represented: a glowing future with the man she loved. Nothing could dent her euphoria.

Rebecca wiped her sweaty palms on her thighs; she had acted on impulse, rushing up to London on a Thursday, hoping to see Benedict. She could not wait till Saturday; she needed reassurance. Sometimes she had to pinch herself to make sure her new-found happiness was true, but this morning she had awakened with a premonition of doom that nothing could dispel.

As the taxi trundled through the London streets she perched on the edge of the seat, her hands tightly clasped to stop them trembling. She was nervous, her stomach full of butterflies. It was stupid, she knew, but she couldn't help herself. She looked at the small diamond ring on the third finger of her left hand, and took a deep, calming breath.

She had come to London shopping—at least that was her excuse. Since their engagement, three weeks ago, she had seen Benedict every weekend, and he regularly telephoned, but somehow they never seemed to get round to discussing a wedding date.

'Here we are, miss.' The taxi driver's voice startled her, and, sitting up straight, she fumbled in her purse for the money he requested.

Handing over a few notes, she said, 'Thank you, and keep the change,' before gathering her parcels and sliding out of the car.

She looked up at the smart white house, the heavy black iron railings and the impressive columns of the portico. In a terrace of similar houses overlooking Regent's Park, 'Nash' if she wasn't mistaken, it was much grander than the apartment she had expected.

What if he wasn't in? she panicked. He had written down his London address the last time they were together, so surely he could not object to her calling?

She held her parcels in front of her like a shield, and, lifting her hand, she pressed the gleaming brass bell. He was her fiancé, for God's sake! What was she worrying about...?

The door swung open and she looked up into the face of a complete stranger. An old man in a dark suit.

'Yes, madam. May I help you?'

'I—I was looking for Benedict Maxwell's apartment,' she stammered, checking once again the slip of paper in her hand.

'Who is it, James?'

It was the right house. 'Your fiancée,' Rebecca sang back, relieved at the sound of Benedict's voice.

'What the hell...?' Benedict appeared. 'It's all right, James, I'll deal with this; you can go on up now, I won't need you any more this evening.'

Rebecca stifled a nervous giggle. A butler called James—she couldn't believe it. Then, raising her eyes, she stared at her fiancé, and hardly recognised him. Just looking at him made her mouth go dry, and set her heart pounding. He was dressed in an immaculate black dinner suit, the jacket a perfect fit, taut across his wide shoulders, a snowy white silk dress shirt contrasting sharply with the polished mahogany colour of his ruggedly attractive face—a testament to his long years in a much warmer climate.

'You'd better come in, Rebecca.'

'Benedict, I thought you lived in an apartment,' she said stupidly as, with a hand at her elbow, he ushered her into a wide marble-floored hall, a beautiful curved staircase the centre-piece.

'In a way I do. The third floor is an apartment for James the butler and his wife—she's my housekeeper.' He stared at her lovely, perplexed face, and noticed her agitation. Almost curtly he said, 'Perhaps you could enlighten me. Why are you here?'

One glance from his dark eyes and Rebecca was putty in his hands. She found herself aching to be held in his arms, to feel his lips on hers, to know the touch of his strong hands on every part of her. The sheer intensity of her passion for him frightened her. She did not know this woman she had become and, worse, she was no longer so sure she knew Benedict.

'Well, I thought I would surprise you; I had some shopping to do.' She held up her parcels and quickly he took them from her hands, and placed them on a convenient table.

'You certainly surprised me, darling, but very pleasantly.' And, dropping a swift kiss on her brow, he placed one arm around her shoulders, and led her through wide double doors into a beautiful room.

'I hope you don't mind, but I thought, as I was in London, I'd take a chance on finding you at home. I know you're coming on Saturday, but I wanted to talk...' She was babbling, and couldn't stop.

'Rebecca, slow down, and sit down,' Benedict commanded sternly. 'Let me get you a drink, and relax. You don't have to explain; as my fiancée you have every right to call on me any time.'

She gulped and sat down on the large velvet sofa Benedict indicated. 'I just wanted to...' But she was talking to his back as he turned to a magnificent polished wood bureau, almost ceiling high, the glass panels tiny diamonds edged in brass instead of the more common lead.

She sank back against the high back of the settee and looked around with interest and amazement. Two long sashed windows let in the early evening sunlight, heavy dark green velvet drapes were caught back with ornate brass holders. Thick oriental carpets covered the magnificently polished strip-wood floor... A globe of the world stood on a small occasional table along with a pile of *National Geographic* magazines—the only sign of disorder in an extremely elegant room.

The walls were covered in pictures, one or two obviously good oil paintings, a few watercolours, and, to her surprise, a large selection of cartoons. A couple of the late Mark Boxer's caricatures caught her eye. She had read of the artist's untimely death from a brain tumour and it had struck a chord in her mind. She recognised the drawings from an article printed in one of the Sunday papers when they were going on auction at Christie's.

'You look rather pensive; thinking of another man, are you?' Benedict's voice cut in on her wayward thoughts. He was at her side, a crystal glass with a good measure of brandy in it held out towards her. 'Or perhaps an old lover?'

'Good heavens, no,' she responded instantly, taking the glass. 'Quite the reverse. I missed you,' she told him honestly. Surely he must be aware of how utterly enslaved she was? Her thinking mind questioned for a second if it was wise to be so dependent on another person for one's happiness, but she quickly dismissed the thought.

She looked up into his dark eyes and her stomach clenched in fear. He looked so intense, as though he could reach down into her mind and read her every thought. Suddenly his mention of a former lover made her wonder again if he had heard about the old scandal. She should have mentioned it, she knew, but somehow the time had never seemed right.

'So,' he said softly, 'you couldn't wait to see me. I'm flattered, darling, and I apologise if I was less than polite when you arrived, but I'll make up for it by taking you out to dinner, hmm?'

He was standing in front of her, his broad shoulders blocking out the light. Impressive didn't begin to de-

scribe him, and she wished he had been casually dressed;
somehow he seemed less approachable in formal clothes.
Strong and powerful, he exuded a raw male virility like
no other man she had ever met. He sparked an instant
reaction inside her that she was helpless to control, didn't
want to...

'I've been tramping around London for hours; I'm
not really dressed for going out.' She looked down at
her now rather crumpled, pretty print summer dress, and
back to his formal attire, and then it hit her. 'I'm sorry.
I should have rung. You are obviously on your way out.'
Why else would he be dressed in an evening suit? she
thought uneasily, and drained her brandy in one gulp,
nervously replacing the glass on a small side-table.

Benedict took a step back and half turned so that his
expression was hidden from her, and she wondered why
she should suddenly feel a chill. She glanced at the
window; had the summer sun gone down? No, but it
was after six in the evening, the warmth had gone. That
must be it...

'No, you're quite wrong. I've only just returned home.
You know how it is—the media are mad keen on en-
vironmental issues, and suddenly I have become flavour
of the month. I've been recording a show for the BBC—
hence the clothes. If you will give me a minute, I'll
change.' He turned and smiled down at her. 'OK?'

Relief flooded through her and her confidence soared.
'I'll come with you,' she teased. 'I wouldn't mind having
a look around your home, I'm already stunned by the
grandeur of the place. I had no idea anthropology paid
so well.'

She did not notice the cynicism in his smile as he held
out his hand and she trustingly put hers in it. He dragged
her to her feet. 'It doesn't. This was my father's house,
and now mine, and I will be delighted to show you
around. You could stay the night.' Golden-brown eyes.

clashed with violet, and for a long, tense moment the air crackled with electric tension.

It was what Rebecca wanted but...

'Your silence is its own answer.' One dark brow arched sardonically. 'You prefer to wait for the band of gold, hmm?'

'No,' she quickly denied. How could she explain her sudden virginal fear? Couldn't he see all she wanted was to be held in his arms and kissed senseless?

For weeks she had been aching with frustration for this man. She would quite happily have gone to bed with him the very first night they met. Instead, apart from a few passionate kisses as he had left her at weekends, they had hardly been alone together.

Benedict rubbed her engagement ring casually with his thumb, his sensuous mouth curved in a knowing smile. His eyes dropped to the soft swell of her breast, the hardening nipples visible beneath the light cotton dress. 'I think I can guess what's on your mind,' he mocked. 'You really are a very precocious young lady, Rebecca, and I might just oblige. I'm only human, and celibacy doesn't suit me either...'

'Oh, Benedict,' she murmured, swaying towards him. 'I came today because I needed to see you, to have your arms around me, to know that what I'm feeling is real and not some dream that will vanish...' She tilted her head, her soft, full lips brushing his, and closed her eyes.

'I thought it was to talk,' he laughed huskily, and her eyes flew open in surprise.

'Yes, that as well,' she admitted ruefully. A stray beam of sunlight glanced across the room, catching Benedict's head, casting strange shadows over the planes and valleys of his strong face. For a second she had the impression of a cynical, ruthless arrogance about him. Far removed from the easygoing, slightly reclusive man she had fallen in love with.

'You're beautiful, Rebecca, and, with your passionate nature, the man isn't born who could refuse you, not want you for his wife.' He said the words almost angrily before bending his dark head, his mouth opening over hers, his tongue pressing against her teeth. Willingly she parted her lips for him, her own tongue tentatively stroking his.

She whimpered as his arm tightened around her back, his mouth suddenly hard and bruising as the kiss deepened into a deep, searching thrust for more. She arched shamelessly against him as his hand stroked down to cup her breast. Benedict groaned deep in his throat, his mouth leaving hers to trail teasingly down the graceful curve of her neck. She slid her small hands inside his jacket, one hand stroking up his broad back, the other roaming lovingly over his muscular chest. She felt the tension in him and rejoiced that she was able to arouse him as instantly as he aroused her.

His hard thighs moved restlessly against her as the hand at her back tangled in her long hair and wrapped it around his wrist. The quick, sharp tug broke through Rebecca's sensual daze.

'Benedict,' she murmured, half protesting, as he held her slightly away from him. The warmth of his breath against her throat, the heavy beat of his heart beneath her small hand, intoxicated her. Surely he felt the same, she thought dizzily. Why was he stopping?

She stared up into his flushed, handsome face. His dark eyes, burning black, fixed on her full, love-swollen lips. 'I will not take you like some love-starved teenager on the living-room floor.'

Daringly she responded, 'So take me upstairs. I'm tired of behaving myself, Benedict. I love you and want you, and we are engaged,' she pleaded shamelessly. Her body ached for him, every hair every pore was sensitised to

his touch, the warmth, the heat of him. She did not think
she could stand any more frustration.

'Do you? I wonder,' he drawled, glancing at her
flushed face before swinging her up in his strong arms.

Rebecca frowned, wondering at the evident cynicism
in his voice; surely he wasn't unsure of her? 'Yes, and
I will always love you,' she told him simply, and, curling
her arms around his wide shoulders, she nuzzled his ear,
as he briskly walked out of the room and up the stairs.

'Can I be sure of that?' he murmured softly, as with
one shoulder he nudged open the door of what was obviously his bedroom.

Rebecca took no notice of her surroundings. Her
whole world was Benedict, and she gazed at him with
wide, wondrous eyes as he laid her down on the huge
bed.

She watched in fascination as he shrugged off his
jacket, his hands going to the buttons of his shirt.

'How many men have drowned in your pansy eyes, I
wonder? You're incredibly beautiful—there must have
been other men in your life. Other loves.' The statement
was really a question, and his dark gaze roamed intently
over her slim, seductive body, coming to rest, with a
strange intensity, on her small face.

Rebecca smiled softly, as realisation struck. He had
asked her before about other men; it was obvious he was
jealous, he needed reassurance, and, dear heaven, she
knew the feeling. Just the thought of any other woman
in Benedict's arms made her feel sick...

'No other men, Benedict, darling, no other love, not
ever,' she murmured, her hands reaching out to him, as
though by touching him she could convince him of the
truth of her words.

His gaze lingered a moment on the garnet glittering
on her finger. 'You sound so positive, so honest,' he
murmured as he finally removed his shirt. 'But surely

you must have had a boyfriend? After all, you are twenty-two; a teenage romance, perhaps?' Something flashed in his eyes, but she didn't notice.

Her hungry gaze was roaming over his naked, hair-roughened chest; his skin gleamed like brown satin in the soft evening light. She watched, mesmerised, as his long fingers dealt expertly with the buckle of his belt, and she gasped as he stepped out of his trousers, the tiny black briefs he wore barely covering his blatant masculinity.

He caught her staring and, lowering himself down on the bed beside her, he arched one brow enquiringly, a teasing smile playing around his sensuous mouth. 'Don't be afraid to confess, darling, I want to know everything about you; the moment I saw you I knew fate had declared we should be together. Nothing you say will make me change my mind, I promise.'

Confess what? she thought, bemused. Oh, yes, boy-friends... His words were all the reassurance she needed; he had fallen in love with her on sight, his feelings were the same as hers, and there should be no secrets between lovers, so dazedly she began to explain, 'There was one young man.' The scandal had upset her father, but she knew Benedict would understand. His hand stroked gently over her knee.

'When?'

'I was seventeen.' His hand slid higher beneath her skirt, and she trembled; all thought of detailed explanations vanished like smoke on the wind, as his seeking fingers stroked the flesh of her inner thigh.

'And?' Benedict rasped as his other hand dealt deftly with the buttons down the front of her dress.

'Nothing,' she groaned. 'He died.'

CHAPTER THREE

HOURS or perhaps only seconds later, they were both naked. Rebecca did not know how or when, because time had ceased to exist. The only reality was Benedict. It had always slightly frightened her, the passion this man aroused in her, but now, in the circle of his embrace, she forgot her fears.

She put her mouth to the hollow of his throat and tasted the tanned flesh, intrigued to realise that his pulse leapt, and the muscular body tensed at her caress; his muffled curse surprised her, but did not deter her. The taste of him, salty and all male, fascinated her, her hand spread out across the soft hair of his chest and traced the narrowing line down his flat stomach. She was lost in a world of the senses, enthralled by the perfection of his male beauty. She felt his stomach muscles clench as her fingers explored lower, learning him by touch.

Rebecca hesitated as he muttered something and groaned, and in a movement that took her by surprise he rolled her over and under him. His mouth trailed a line of fire down her throat to her breast, and a shocked gasp escaped her. Then his large body blocked the evening light, and for a second she feared the huge, dark shadow blotting out the world; then his hand cupped her breast and his mouth closed over one rosy nipple, tasting and suckling the hard tip.

Her body arched in a spasm of delight, every nerve quivering and tightening to an aching tension. She felt the heat of his body and with trembling hands she reached out and stroked the shape of him from chest to thigh.

'I want you, I can't help it.' Benedict's guttural moan vibrated across her heart as his mouth teased each breast in turn.

She whimpered tiny little erotic cries of keen encouragement. She was swamped by the force of her own latent sensuality which she had never known she possessed. His strong hands caressed her burning flesh, finding the secret, hidden temple of her womanhood, stroking the hot, moist, sensitive flesh.

Nothing in her life so far had prepared her for such a tumult of erotic sensations. Her body welcomed and gloried at his touch and feverishly she sought to return the ecstasy. Her slender fingers slid across his thigh, cupping the maleness of him in a bold caress. She felt his muscles lock rigid in an attempt to restrain his response, then his hand tore hers from his body, pinning it above her head in one violent motion.

'God forgive me, Gor——'

A swift stab of pain and she cried out, her slender body clenching for an instant in rejection as he made her his with one powerful thrust.

'No, no, I don't believe...' Benedict grated.

But Rebecca, the pain subsiding, was drowning in a hot molten flood of desire. She clung to his broad shoulders, her fingernails digging into his flesh, while her body sheathed the strength and force of his masculinity, knowing and welcoming its master.

Benedict stilled, every muscle in his large frame locked in an intolerable tension; she looked up into his tight, darkly flushed face and begged, 'Don't stop. Please...'

Her words unleashed a wild, savage passion that should have terrified her; instead she met him thrust for thrust. She was swept along in a maelstrom of emotion, and she clung to him, her slender legs wrapped around his waist, as he took her higher and higher; she could sense the awaiting pinnacle, and cried out as the tension almost tore her apart.

She sobbed his name, the world exploding around her as he took her with him into the swirling vortex. He touched her womb, his harsh, guttural groan swallowed by her mouth, as the liquid of life flowed between them. She knew he had captured the very essence of her being and absorbed her into him. They were one...

Rebecca had read about sex, but nothing in the world had prepared her for the reality. It wasn't possible, she thought, her body trembling in the aftermath of release, that any other two people in the universe could experience what had passed between herself and Benedict. His head lay on her shoulder, great, shuddering breaths racking his huge frame. She reached a hand to stroke the hair from his damp brow to tell him her thoughts.

He raised his head and caught her wrist, holding it with a grip of steel. His breathing slowly returning to normal, he said with barely contained rage, 'You were a virgin. Damn you to hell, Rebecca!' And, rolling off her, he swung his feet to the floor, presenting her with his back.

Her new-found euphoria dwindled beneath his hostile words. What had happened? Why did he resent the fact she had been a virgin? It didn't make sense. Pulling herself up into a sitting position, she tentatively reached out a hand to his stiff back. 'What's wrong?' she asked softly, fearfully.

At the touch of her fingers, he jumped up and swung around to face her; totally unconscious of his own nudity, he stared down at her with dark, hostile eyes. 'I guessed you were evil, but my God, to think Gordon, the poor sod, went to his grave never knowing what it was like to have a woman. What did you do, string him along

with a few kisses until he was out of his mind with
wanting you?'

Rebecca shivered, not with cold, but with the slow,
icy chill that crawled up her spine and encircled her heart.
'I don't understand,' she whispered; her violet eyes lifted
to his and fell beneath the blazing anger she saw registered there.

'That's right, hang your head in shame, you bitch!'

His scathing words cut her like a whip, but bravely
she raised her head. She still wasn't sure what had happened, but the mention of Gordon filled her with fore-
boding. She could explain that episode in her life;
Benedict would understand, she told herself. He loved
her and she had done nothing wrong.

'What was it the papers called you? A pint-sized
Lolita. A pocket Venus.' His gaze ran the length of her
naked body, blatant with contempt. Rebecca held her
head high, and with trembling hands she brushed the
tumbled mass of her black hair over her shoulders. She
was too shocked to speak. She said nothing. Earlier she
had been going to explain her one unfortunate relationship, but Benedict's persuasive, sophisticated lovemaking had washed the thought from her head. Now it
was too late...

His dark eyes followed the movements of her hands
then settled insolently on her bare breasts before slowly
rising to her pale face. 'I have to agree with them. On
the outside you are everything a man could want—intelligent, beautiful, perfectly formed and passionate—
but inside, where it counts, you have none of the female
virtues, no warmth, no compassion.'

She looked at him, the man she loved, the man she
had given everything to only moments earlier, and did
not recognise him. Her eyes roamed over his large, still
sweat-wet body; she had traced those muscles with her
fingers, kissed those lips. She shook her head to dispel

the image. This towering naked man, bristling with hostility, was a stranger. How could he turn on her so?

'Nothing to say, Rebecca, no defence?'

'I didn't think I would need to defend myself to my fiancé,' she said bleakly. 'I thought you of all people, Benedict, wouldn't believe the gutter Press, and anyway it all happened years ago. I was barely eighteen.' She wondered how he had found out. Not that it mattered. It was enough that he had, and immediately thought the worst of her. She had expected better from the man she loved.

Benedict laughed, a harsh, guttural sound. 'The Press do exaggerate occasionally, but my own mother showed me Gordon's diary—his last entry before he died.'

'Your mother?' she murmured. What in God's name had his mother got to do with it? She was totally confused.

'Yes, Rebecca. Gordon Brown was my half-brother and you destroyed him,' he said with pitiless certainty.

Rebecca moaned, a soft, low sound; suddenly Benedict's actions made a horrible kind of sense.

'Now I think you're beginning to understand...Rebecca.' He drawled her name. 'Derived from the Hebrew. Charmer. Ensnarer. Tell me, my love, my fiancée, how does it feel to be the one ensnared for a change?' he demanded malevolently.

How does it feel? The question echoed in her head. As though she were breaking into a million pieces, she thought. But she would not give Benedict the satisfaction of knowing how close he had come to destroying her. Slowly she turned and slid her trembling legs over the opposite edge of the bed from him, she grabbed the edge of the sheet and wrapped it around her numb body, and, with a terrific effort of will, she rose to her feet. Only then did she turn to face him, the wide, rumpled bed between them.

'The coroner's verdict was accidental death,' she said
softly. Why was he blaming her? She had been completely innocent of any involvement.

'Yes, but we both know why—to save embarrassment
to a good Catholic family. Mother never showed the
court the diary, her young son's outpouring of a hopeless
love. You were leaving him the following day, and would
never wear his ring.'

Benedict walked around the bed and snatched her left
hand in his, his thumb rubbing her engagement ring. He
watched her, a strange, feral glitter in his golden-brown
eyes. She looked down at their joined hands.

'Gordon bought the ring for you years ago, but you
wouldn't take it from him. Ironic, isn't it? You almost
snatched my hand off when-I gave it to you,' he drawled
cynically. 'But then you love me; I should be flattered.'
With his free hand he tilted her chin, forcing her to look
at him. 'Isn't that so, Rebecca?'

She flushed with humiliation at the taunting words.
'No.' She breathed the lie. She loved Benedict, not this
vengeful stranger. How could she love this man when
his hatred of her was blatant in his every glance?

The taut muscles of his hard body flexed at her denial,
and his hands dropped from her, as though her touch
were somehow contaminating. She could feel the anger
emanating from him and, pulling the sheet closer round
her small frame, she tucked it sarong-style beneath her
armpits, and stepped back only to find her feet hopelessly tangled in the trailing silk and herself tumbling
forward.

Benedict's strong hands caught her and held her steady
against the hard warmth of his naked body.

'Actions speak louder than words, darling, and what
your lips deny, your body aches for,' he said with harsh
triumph, his insolent gaze dropping to her full breasts,

the hard nipples clearly outlined against the soft silk of the sheet.

Scarlet-faced, she tried to push him away. 'No.'

'Not fifteen minutes ago you were begging me to love you. Now I think you might appreciate and begin to feel some of the anguish my brother felt when you refused his love,' Benedict said gloatingly, and, lifting her up as though she weighed no more than a feather, he dropped her back down on the bed.

'Stay there and think about it while I shower and dress. Then we'll talk.' The last sounded like a threat.

Rebecca had to get away... to think... She jumped up and in a frantic scramble around the floor found her panties and bra, then she quickly struggled into her clothes. It had all gone so horribly wrong; her premonition of doom that had sent her running to London had proved to be true. She was hurting too much to think clearly, but she knew she had made a complete and utter fool of herself.

Benedict was right when he said she had almost snatched his hand off to wear his ring; she cringed at the memory. The happenings of the last few weeks ran through her mind like an express train, and in a flash of blinding clarity she saw it all. Benedict did not love her, never had, even the act of love they had shared was false. She remembered his, 'God forgive me,' or had it been 'Gordon'? He had never wanted to make love to her, she had thrown herself at him.

With fingers that shook she fastened the last button on her print dress, then carefully removed the ring from the third finger of her left hand. With it went all her hopes and dreams of love and marriage.

She raised her head as Benedict sauntered back into the room. He looked magnificent; his dark hair, wet from the shower, was swept back smoothly from his broad forehead. He had slipped on a blue cotton velour jogging

suit, and the pants clung lovingly to his muscular thighs,
subtly outlining his virile masculinity.

Rebecca flushed, her stomach clenching in pain for
what she had lost. But self-pity had always been an
emotion she despised. So she choked down her emotions
and proudly raised her eyes to his. She held out her hand,
the ring nestling in her palm.

'You can have this back. I understand perfectly,
Benedict.' He had wanted revenge and he had used her
to get it.

'Good God, no, you keep that little bauble; it was
meant for you. If I ever give a woman a ring it would
be worth a hell of a lot more than that.'

Rebecca glanced at his arrogant, taunting face. Dear
heaven, what a fool she had been. How had she never
noticed the cruel twist to his mouth, the ruthless element
in his nature? She hadn't because she had been blinded
by love...

She could not look at him, it hurt too much. Slowly
she let her gaze roam around the room. The lavish
drapes, the inches-thick cream carpet, and, lastly, the
enormous bed. It was like the rest of the house, elegant
and very expensive. She did not fit here, never would.
Her fingers closed over the ring in her hand; Gordon
had never told her about the ring, but then he wouldn't
have, not when he'd found out. He would have wanted
to spare her the pain of losing him. Her lips curled in a
soft smile. He had been that sort of boy. Always caring
for others.

'Rebecca.' Benedict touched her shoulder. She
stiffened.

'Don't touch me.' She raised moisture-glazed eyes to
his. 'You're wrong about one thing, Benedict. Gordon
bought this ring with love in his heart; any ring you gave
a woman would be worth nothing in comparison. You
don't have a heart.'

She had the consolation of seeing his face darken with barely controlled anger. 'You dare say that to me? I read Gordon's last entry in his diary, and I quote.'

In a voice laced with cynicism he continued.

Becky, I love her. Sweet Becky. But I know now she will never wear my ring. She burns like the brightest star in the heavens, a brilliant future awaits her. While for me life is over.

'The poor fool was besotted by you, and you killed him as surely as if you had stuck a knife in him. Don't talk to me about heart,' he sneered. 'You don't know the meaning of the word. But by God, I am going to teach you.'

Rebecca brushed the back of her hand across her eyes, whipping away the tears, deeply touched by the quotation. But what did he mean, he was going to teach her?

'I don't think so,' she said quietly. She wanted nothing more to do with the man. She stepped around him, heading for the door, and escape. She felt as though she were living through a nightmare and if she did not get away soon she might break down completely. She was teetering on the edge.

Think practically, she told herself, opening the door. If she hurried she could catch the last train to Oxford.

'Where are you going?' The staccato question halted her in mid-stride. 'I haven't finished with you yet.'

Slowly she turned and looked back at Benedict. 'Yes. Yes, you have.' In a couple of strides he was beside her; reaching out, he caught a handful of her long hair. 'Let go of me,' she said tightly, 'I have a train to catch.'

His sensuous mouth curved in a knowing smile. 'But you wanted to stay the night, Rebecca,' he mocked. 'You want me, you know you do.'

She wrenched away from him, and when he made to follow her she turned on him, her violet eyes blazing with anger. 'I've heard of mad scientists but you beat the lot,' she said scathingly. 'I wouldn't want you if you were the last man on earth.'

To her astonishment he laughed. 'That might be awkward, as we are engaged to be married.'

She glanced up at him; his golden-brown eyes shone with mockery and something else she did not recognise. Then the full extent of her stupidity hit her. Engaged? What a joke! 'You never intended to marry me, did you?'

His dark eyes narrowed on her pale face. 'I never actually asked you, so what do you think?' he responded mockingly.

Rebecca, shamed, could not answer. She knew, and, swinging on her heel, she walked along the hall and downstairs. Mechanically she picked up the parcels from the hall table, and left the ring. Benedict's hand on her arm stopped her at the front door.

'Wait. You can't wander around London at night. I'll drive you to the station,' he said curtly.

She sat in the far corner of the seat, as far away from Benedict as she could get. She felt like ranting and raving, screaming her anguish to the world, but instead she clenched her hands in her lap, her knuckles white with the strain. She would not give the swine the satisfaction of knowing how he had hurt her.

'I'll drive you back to Oxford,' Benedict said, breaking the icy silence.

'No, thank you. I have my rail ticket.'

'So what? It will be quicker by car.' He shot her a sidelong glance, a grim smile twisting his lips. 'I don't mind the drive.'

The conceit of the man, the arrogance, amazed her. 'Well, I do,' she fired back. 'The quicker I get away from your hateful presence, the better I will like it,' she said through clenched teeth.

His strong hands tightened on the driving-wheel, as he spun the car in a quick arc and headed for the station. 'I take it by that comment you're breaking our engagement?' he enquired, flashing her a brief, oddly intense glance.

With bitter cynicism she answered him, using his own earlier words, 'What do you think?'

He brought the big car to a halt in the station forecourt. Rebecca reached for the door-handle.

'Rebecca, wait.' Turning in the seat, he caught her by the shoulders, his dark eyes searching her small face. 'I never intended ...' He hesitated. She had never seen him uncertain before, and, for all her desire to escape, she did wait.

'I didn't mean it to end like this, and well ... If there are any repercussions ... I'll help you.'

A hysterical laugh escaped her. Repercussions? Who was he kidding? She would be suffering from this night for the rest of her life. 'Thanks, but no, thanks.'

'I insist Rebecca; if you are pregnant I want to know.'

What little colour she had left vanished. How could she have been so dumb? Dredging up every last ounce of will-power she possessed, she stared straight into his dark eyes and lied her head off. 'Really, Benedict, I know I might have given you the impression to the contrary, but I'm not a complete idiot. You said yourself once that I was a great organiser. I started taking the Pill weeks ago. You have nothing to worry about.' Not waiting for his response, she opened the door and slid out of the car.

Benedict made no attempt to stop her. She walked quickly away, stiff-backed with her head held high, and she never looked back. Please God, she prayed, give me strength. Let me get on this train and home before I fall apart.

She sat huddled against the window of the train, staring out into the darkness, the lights of the city flashing and dazzling her eyes. She was in a state of shock, totally numb, but she knew that somewhere in the dark shadows of her mind lurked an agony not to be borne. Her thoughts slid back in time, a sad, reminiscent smile quirking her full lips. Gordon Brown, poor gentle, caring Gordon, he would have been horrified to know how Benedict had used his ring...

It had been the summer before she started university. Her father had taken a holiday home for six weeks at Sidmouth in Devon. The small seaside town was renowned for holding the best folk festival in England every summer, and her father had been a devotee of folk music.

It had been the middle of July, the first week of their holiday, when Rebecca had met Gordon Brown. She had been walking along the water's edge, enjoying the sun and sea, when she was almost hit by the boom of a sailing dinghy swinging around in the wind; she had ducked just in time but fallen on her backside on the hard pebble beach.

A young man, a tall, golden-haired Adonis, had dashed out of the water and helped her to her feet, and that had been the start of their friendship. He had told her he was a first-year student at Essex University, and he had kidded her about her being a brain-box when she had shyly informed him she was going up to Oxford in September.

Over the following weeks they had spent almost every day together. He had taught her to crew the dinghy for him, they had walked for miles around the headlands, lunched in excellent little restaurants in the small but beautiful villages of Seaton and Beer, and generally enjoyed themselves. Gordon's pride and joy was a little red Mini car and in it they had travelled over Dartmoor, and all the surrounding countryside.

She rarely, if ever, saw him in the evenings; those were devoted to his mother. He had asked her once or twice to join them, but she refused. Her own evenings were reserved for her father.

Looking back, she realised he had not said much about his family—only that his mother was French but had spent most of her life in England, as his father had been English. Gordon was holidaying with her mainly because both his father and his older half-brother had died the previous year and his mother was completely devastated and needed his loving care. Gordon confessed he missed his father, but he had never been very close to his brother, so it had not affected him as much as his mother.

It had been the last week of August and almost the end of the holiday when the tragedy happened. With hindsight Rebecca recognised all the signs had been there, but she was too young to realise it at the time. On the Monday, she had not seen Gordon—he had had business in London—but on the Tuesday they went sailing and he had caught his head a nasty crack on the boom.

Laughing, she had told him he should be more careful or get a bigger dinghy, if he wanted to keep his head, but he had not laughed. Instead he had said quite soberly, 'A crack on the head won't make any difference to me now, Becky; the damage is done.'

Rebecca had wondered what he meant, but hadn't bothered querying his statement. It had been a beautiful day, a day out of time; they had tied the boat up at a little cove and picnicked on the beach. After they had eaten they lay side by side on the blanket, and for the first time, Rebecca had some inkling of the depths of

Gordon's feelings for her. Oh, they had exchanged kisses once or twice, but that was all.

This day was different. He leaned over her, his boyish face oddly serious, his golden-brown eyes dulled with a haunting sadness.

'Becky, I want you to know the past few weeks have been the most perfect of my life, and if circumstances had been different——'

'Gordon, why so serious?' she cut in, not sure what to say to him. 'I've promised to spend tomorrow with Dad. We're going fossicking at Lyme Regis, but we will still have another day before I leave. And after that we can write to each other; I'll persuade my father to come back next year.'

Gordon smiled a truly beautiful smile then very gently kissed her lips. 'Yes, Becky, you do that.' And somehow in that moment he had seemed much older than his years.

A sigh escaped her. She could understand his entry in the diary that last day. He had known he was terminally ill and had obviously decided he could not give her the ring, with the commitment it implied. He was too caring to burden her with his problem.

She rested her head against the back of the seat, closing her eyes. The regular, rhythmic beat of the train was oddly soothing. It had all been so long ago, and she had thought the episode was forgotten, until tonight and Benedict.

She had never seen Gordon again. The following day she had spent with her dad, and, on returning to their apartment on the seafront at Sidmouth late in the afternoon, she had been accosted by a complete stranger. Before she knew what was happening a flash bulb had gone off in her face, and a horrible little man was flinging questions at her.

'Gordon Brown was your boyfriend. Had you fought with him? Was that why he was on his own today? Do you think he drove over the cliff deliberately? Was his death suicide?'

Rebecca had been stunned and completely numb; the staccato questions rained down on her like machine-gun bullets. She had no idea what she replied, and was grateful for her father's support as he hustled her into the apartment.

It had been a twenty-four-hour sensation at the time, created by one of the most disreputable newspapers. A photo of Rebecca, her long hair tumbling about her face in disarray, and dressed in scanty shorts and sun-top, had appeared on the front page. WAS IT ACCIDENT OR SUICIDE? the headline screamed, and they had dubbed her a 'pint-sized Lolita'.

The irony of it still made her smart. When the inquest was held a week later, the verdict was accidental death. The same newspaper printed the result in three sentences on page twenty-one. Her father had attended the inquest and told her about it afterwards.

Poor Gordon, Becky thought sadly, he had never stood a chance. The coroner's report had explained everything. Gordon had attended the medical centre at the university in May, complaining of headaches. Tests had been carried out and a massive brain tumour diagnosed. The Monday before his death he had visited a specialist in London, only to be told it was inoperable. He had known he was going to die. The pathologist's report had confirmed that Gordon had suffered a massive brain haemorrhage and in all likelihood was dead before his car went over the cliff.

An elderly couple who had been talking to him only minutes before confirmed he had complained the sun was giving him a headache and he was going home. They had watched him get into the little Mini, and it was obvious he was about to reverse away from the edge of the headland, as his arm was along the back of the passenger-seat, and he was looking behind him. But for some inexplicable reason he missed the gear and the car slid forward and over the cliff.

'My dear, are you all right?'

Rebecca's eyes flew open, and hastily she brushed a tear from her cheek as her startled gaze settled on the lady seated opposite her on the train.

'Yes, yes, thank you,' she murmured, jolted back to the present by the old lady's intervention.

'Are you sure? You look very pale.'

'Yes, I'm sure,' she responded, trying to smile. She wished she were home in the safety of her own bedroom, but she had to hang on for a while longer...

CHAPTER FOUR

QUIETLY Rebecca let herself into the house and tiptoed up the stairs. It was well past midnight but, with a baby in the house, one never knew at what hour of the night Mary or Rupert would be up, and the last thing she wanted was to bump into either of them.

She closed the bedroom door behind her and slumped against it, her handbag and parcels dropped unheeded at her feet. With hands that shook she unbuttoned her dress and let it fall to the floor, then, walking like an old woman, she crossed the room and collapsed on the small bed.

Like a small, wounded animal, she crawled under the coverlet, burrowing down in the bed to hide. She pulled the pillow down with her and, gripping it tightly, she buried her head in the soft down and finally let the tears fall.

She cried and cried, great, gulping sobs that shook her small body from head to toe, the sound muffled by the soft pillow. How long she cried, she had no idea, until at last, her throat raw, her eyes dry, her slender frame ceased shuddering; but the pain, the hurt, it went on and on...

Slowly she turned on her back and, pushing the pillow under her aching head, she gazed with dull, sightless eyes at the ceiling.

Benedict Maxwell, the man she had loved, had hoped to marry, was responsible for her agony of mind and body, and the worst part was knowing he had acted with a brutal, cold-blooded deliberation to achieve just this result.

The first time she set eyes on him, Rebecca had thought she had met her soulmate. What a fool she had been! Of course Benedict had seemed familiar. Why wouldn't he? His golden eyes were exactly the same as his younger half-brother's had been. If she had not been so smitten, so damned gullible, her analytical mind might have recognised the likeness earlier. Instead she had dreamt of love and happy-ever-after.

Rebecca groaned; thinking clearly for the first time in hours, she cringed at her own stupidity. It was all so obvious. Benedict had barely noticed her when they were first introduced. It was only when Rupert gave her full name that Benedict had turned the potent force of his masculine charm upon her.

The next day Mary had tried to warn her, and Rebecca, in her conceit, had told her, 'Deep down I know he's the one for me, and if I get hurt, so be it.' How prophetic those words had been. The same night, on her first dinner date with Benedict, he had asked her about any other admirers, and she had eagerly avowed he was the one and only man for her. At the time she had wondered why he had said he would believe her 'for the moment'. Bitterly she realised he had been stringing her along to cause her the maximum pain, and she, dear heaven, had helped him. So many comments she had dismissed as irrelevant now made horrible sense.

Rebecca moved restlessly; she longed for the oblivion of sleep, anything to stop the memories, but it was not to be. Her mind spun on oiled wheels, recalling every word every gesture of her time with Benedict. Her body burnt with aching frustration, never to know the touch of his hands, the warmth of his lips, the ecstasy of his possession. How could she survive without him?

If only he had not made love to her, she thought bitterly. The agony of having known the wonder of being his completely, only to discover he cared nothing for her, had forced himself to take what she had so blatantly offered, tore at the very heart of her womanhood, destroyed her pride.

The grey light of dawn was lighting the sky, when she finally faced the most crushing, humiliating fact of all: she was partly to blame for the situation she now had to endure. Benedict was wrong about her relationship with his brother, wrong about her. But one comment he had made was perfectly true, and she could not deny it. He had never actually asked her to marry him. He had given her the ring, and she had immediately jumped to the conclusion that he was proposing marriage. She had even felt touched because he had avoided her eyes, and she had assumed he was nervous.

Her shame and humiliation were complete. No wonder he'd been in no hurry to fix the wedding day. He had never intended to marry her. He'd wanted revenge for his brother and she, fool that she was, had given him the rope to hang her by.

A baby's cry broke the morning silence. Rebecca stiffened where she lay. Young Jonathan was making his wants known. She glanced at her watch. Dead on time. Six-thirty every morning, the little one awoke, demanding his feed.

She could hear Mary moving around in the room across the hall, and knew she could not delay the inevitably painful discussion much longer.

Half an hour later, she swung her legs over the side of the bed and stood up. She lifted her slender arms over her head and stretched. Rebecca winced and dropped her hands, her muscles aching in places they never had before. Determinedly she convinced herself it was the result of her sleepless night and had absolutely nothing whatsoever to do with Benedict's passionate love-making. No, she corrected, there had been no love on his part.

Pulling on her old towelling robe, she gathered up bra, panties, a pair of jeans and a sweater, and headed along the hall for the bathroom. Safely behind the locked door, she stripped and stepped into the shower-stall. Turning on the tap, she turned her face up to the warm spray, letting the water wash over her. Picking up a bar of toilet soap, she lathered her slender body from top to toe. Her long hair trailed in black tails down her back, as over and over again she repeated the process in a feverish attempt to wash every touch, every lingering scent of Benedict from her flesh.

A knock on the bathroom door brought an end to her frantic washing. A wry smile curved her full lips. That would be Rupert. It was a lovely old house Mary and Rupert had intended modernising but, as Rupert had been offered a post at Harvard in the USA, starting in the autumn, they had postponed any renovations; hence one bathroom was shared by all.

Benedict must have really felt he was slumming it, staying here, she thought bitterly, memories of his elegant home fresh in her mind. Obviously he had been prepared to put up with any inconvenience in order to carry out his scheme to hurt her.

Bile rose in her throat, and for an instant she thought she was going to be sick as she recognised just how deviously Benedict had behaved. Fighting down her nausea, she quickly rubbed herself dry with a large fluffy towel. A slow-burning, bitter anger took root in her mind as she hastily donned her clothes. He had used her friends, the ring, anything and anyone, in order to break her heart.

Rebecca stood in front of the washbasin and neatly wrapped a towel round her soaking hair, turban style.

She stared at her pale, hollow-eyed reflection and made a silent vow. Neither Benedict Maxwell nor anyone else would ever know just how well he had succeeded. It would be hard, but for her own pride, her self-respect, not by a look or a word would she ever betray how much he had hurt her.

She thought of her late father. He had fought a killing illness with spirit and determination; surely she could do as well with an unfortuante love-affair? The hardest thing to accept was, she was as guilty as Benedict in a way. She had not behaved very intelligently and now she was paying the price.

She opened the door. 'It's all yours, Rupert,' she told him, and ran downstairs.

She straightened her shoulders and hesitated for a second outside the kitchen door. It was about to begin. She walked into the homely room. Mary was seated by the kitchen table, on a low nursing chair, feeding Jonathan. She raised her head and smiled, but at the sight of Rebecca the smile quickly turned to a frown.

'Really, Becky, you should have stayed in bed. You look haggard as hell. What time did you get back last night?'

'Thanks Mary, and good morning to you too,' Rebecca muttered as she walked across the room and, leaning against the pine work-top, switched on the kettle. 'Coffee?' she prompted, her back to Mary.

'It's ready in the percolator.'

'Oh, thanks.' The percolator sat in the middle of the kitchen table, two cups beside it. Carefully she poured out a cup of coffee, willing her hand not to shake, then, with apparent nonchalance, she pulled out one of the ladder-backed chairs and sat down facing Mary. 'How is hungry Horace this morning, my favourite godson?' she asked with a smile for the tiny bundle lying in his mother's arms, determinedly gulping down his bottle of formula. Mary had given up breast-feeding the week before.

'A hell of a lot better than you.' Mary's blue eyes searched Rebecca's face. 'You look as though you haven't slept a wink. Nothing wrong, is there?'

She could think of no easy way to say it. 'The engagement is off.'

Mary jerked upright and young Jonathan yelled as his bottle fell out of his mouth. 'Off? What do you mean, off?'

'I'm sorry, Mary, I know I've caused you a lot of trouble, Benedict staying here and everything, but the engagement was a mistake.' She did not want to explain the true reason, but she owed Mary some explanation. 'I met him yesterday in London, and we had a long talk and agreed we were incompatible.'

'Just like that? But Rebecca——'

'No, Mary, I really don't want to discuss it,' She cut her off bluntly, and, draining her cup of coffee, she stood up. 'If you don't mind I'd like to use the phone in the study. I know I said I would help you with the baby, but would you mind terribly if I went away for a while? I thought I might go and stay with Josh and Joanne if they'll have me.'

'Of course I don't mind, Becky; you look as if you could use a holiday. But don't you think you're being a little hasty? Take it from me, I know—one fight doesn't mean you have to break up. I bet Benedict will be here any minute, full of apologies.'

'It's no good, Mary, my mind is made up. Just take my word for it.'

Maybe it was something in Rebecca's tone but Mary stared at her, her smooth brow drawn in a deep frown. 'I think you really mean that.' She hesitated, her sharp eyes surveying the young girl standing so stiffly before

her. 'If you didn't fight...it must have... Wait a minute.
You were late last night.'

Rebecca could almost see the older woman's brain
ticking over, but she could do nothing to enlighten her.
Then, to her stunned amazement, Mary blushed.

'I know, Rebecca. You were a virgin, and last night
you and Benedict...'

Now it was Rebecca's turn to blush.

'Oh, you poor girl,' Mary went on. 'You made love
and bells didn't ring. That's it, isn't it? But it's no reason
to break up. The first time is quite often less than perfect
for any woman. Not everyone clicks in the sexual stakes
immediately; with some couples it takes time. Don't be
put off, Benedict will soon teach——'

'Mary, you don't understand.' Rebecca couldn't listen
to any more. 'I don't want Benedict. Is that plain
enough?' she said sharply, and was immediately contrite. 'Sorry, Mary, but trust me—I know what I'm
doing. And if you'll excuse me, right now I have a call
to make.' Head up, she walked stiffly out of the kitchen
and across the hall to the study.

It hardly seemed possible that one's life could change
so drastically in twenty-four hours, Rebecca thought
wearily. She sat down at the leather-topped desk, and,
resting her elbows on the desk, she propped her head in
her hands and gazed vacantly into space.

With hindsight it was glaringly obvious that Benedict
had no intention of committing himself to her. He had
never introduced her to a single friend of his, and there
must be plenty. Carefully making sure only to visit her
at her home, only mixing with her acquaintances...so
only Rebecca was humiliated...

Wearily she straightened and picked up the telephone.
Joanne and Josh, pals from college and now husband
and wife and living in Northumbria. They had been so
pleased for her when she had last called, and told them

she was engaged. How would they react when she told them it was off? And could they put up with a visitor for a few weeks? she thought wryly.

Rebecca need not have worried; once she had spoken to Joanne it was all arranged. With a relieved sigh she carefully replaced the receiver. Now all she had to do was pack her bags and drive off...

A light knock on the door heralded the arrival of a very worried-looking Mary, carrying a tray with coffee and biscuits on it. 'I thought you might need something, love,' she said, placing the tray on the desk.

Need... What she needed was a time machine to whisk her back a couple of months, but failing that a strong coffee would have to suffice. 'Thanks,' she murmured, taking the cup from her friend's outstretched hand.

'Are you sure you know what you're doing, Rebecca?'

'Yes, very sure. I can't explain now, but perhaps some day. I only know Benedict Maxwell is not the man I thought he was, not the man I thought I loved. You and Rupert were both right—you told me at the very beginning to be careful. I should have listened...'

The phone rang, a jarring sound beside the soft voices. 'I'll get that.' Mary jumped to answer it. 'You've had enough.'

More than enough. How long she could hang on to her sanity, she did not know. She tensed.

'Yes, I'm sorry, Ben, but Rebecca has been using the phone.'

Rebecca carefully bent forward and placed her coffee-cup on the floor, the action easing the swift stab of pain she felt in her stomach as she realised it was Benedict calling. Taking a deep, calming breath, she straightened up.

'Becky——' Mary held the phone out '—it's Benedict. He wants to talk to you.'

The swine, the arrogant, heartless swine. How dared he ring her now? Hadn't he hurt her enough? she thought furiously. She had just spent the most humiliating few hours of her life, and all because of him. She jumped to her feet, violet eyes blazing. 'Well, tell Mr Benedict Maxwell I do not wish to speak to him, see him or hear his name mentioned ever again.'

'I guess you heard that, Ben.'

Rebecca didn't know what Benedict replied and didn't want to. But she hesitated on her way to the door at Mary's cry of outrage.

'Ben, I have a young baby in the house; he is asleep at the moment and I want him to stay that way. You can't keep ringing all day and night.'

Rebecca marched over to the desk and snatched the phone from Mary's hand. 'Yes, Mr Maxwell?''

'Really, Rebecca, surely you know me well enough— especially after last night—to call me Benedict.'

His mocking response was just what she needed to hold on to her anger. 'On the contrary, Mr Maxwell, last night showed me I didn't know you at all,' she declared icily, as the door closed on Mary's exit.

'Lying naked in my arms, making those erotic little whimpering noises, you quite happily called my name. I seem to remember you begging me to get to know you completely,' Benedict drawled throatily, the amusement evident in his tone.

Stamping down on the sensual images his words evoked, she replied, 'Was there something you particularly wanted, or do you just like making obscene phone calls? If that is the case I suggest you choose a number at random and stop bothering me.'

'Do I bother you, Rebecca?'

'Not any more. And by the way I have told Mary the engagement is off, but perhaps you would like to stick a notice in *The Times*,' she said sarcastically. She

wouldn't put it past the devil to make her humiliation
as public as possible.

'That was what I wanted to talk about,' Benedict vol-
unteered, the amusement vanished from his voice. 'I had
hoped to catch you before... Well, anyway, what I mean
Rebecca, is there is no reason to break our engagement.
I thought about it al—last night, and I realised maybe
I overreacted a bit.'

She gasped her astonishment. What the hell was he
playing at now? He actually sounded contrite.

'I realised I can't blame you alone for Gordon's death.'

For a moment Rebecca's heart soared—he had discovered the truth—but as he continued she turned from
white to pink to red with fury.

'After all, you were very young. Young girls do flirt.
You probably didn't realise how much a man feels in
certain situations. You were still a virgin, a very beautiful, romantic young girl. You probably didn't realise
what a tease——'

'Stop right there.' Rebecca snapped. He actually had
the colossal nerve, the arrogance, to try to make excuses
for her...

'I have heard quite enough. We are finished. *Kaputt
Finito*. And as for you...I suggest you take yourself
back to the Amazon and your half-baked theories of my
character with you, and stuff them where the monkey
stuffed his nuts. In future you would do better to stick
to the study of primitive tribes—you're obviously on the
same wavelength.'

His laughter had her clenching her fists with anger.

'Crude, Rebecca, crude... Though it doesn't surprise
me—you always were a little firecracker, and now I know
you give the same explosive response in bed. I can't help
thinking, Gordon aside, you and I could have a very
fruitful adult relationship.'

Benedict was certainly showing his true colours now, she thought sadly, all her rage evaporating like air out of a burst balloon. The conceit of the man—he would kindly overlook the fact that he thought she was responsible for his brother's death for a bit of good old-fashioned lust. He hadn't a decent principle in his whole body, and she had been a complete and utter fool to think otherwise.

'Why have you called, Benedict? To gloat,' she answered her own question.

Perhaps the blunt finality in her tone got through to Benedict, or maybe he had lost interest in goading her, because his reply was voiced with a cool formality. 'No, Rebecca. When you were sitting on the train last night, I thought you looked rather upset. I only called to assure myself you got home safely.'

'Thank you for your concern, but it was quite unnecessary,' she drawled sarcastically. 'Goodbye.' And, slamming down the receiver, she gripped the edge of the desk with her small hands, her head bowed as she fought to retain her self-control. Her legs were trembling, barely able to support her.

Eventually regaining some semblance of control, she went looking for Mary, and found her in the kitchen. 'It's arranged. I'm going to Corbridge for a while.'

'Yes, love, It will do you good to get away. But you know we're here if you need us.'

'Thanks.' Rebecca's violet eyes glazed with tears. Thank God she had friends like Mary and Rupert. 'I don't know what I would do without you and Rupert.'

'Hey, come on, Becky. What are friends for? Only don't forget to come back for the last Sunday of August—Jonathan's christening.'

'As if I would,' she smiled through her tears.

*   *   *

Rebecca slid into the driving-seat of the Ford Sierra, and,
with her suitcase stowed in the back, and explicit in-
structions on how to get to Corbridge, she waved
goodbye to Mary and started the engine. Some seven
hours later, with her head aching, she saw the welcoming sign of the village on the roadside.

She drove into the little market square. At one end
was an old stone church, and the other three sides were
a mixture of houses and shops and, luckily, a parking
space.

Josh and Joanne lived in a teetering three-storeyed
house overlooking the square, and just as Rebecca raised
her hand to press the bell the door was flung open and,
in a flurry of embraces, she was dragged enthusiastically
into the house. It had been over a year since their last
meeting at a party in Oxford to celebrate the end of their
university years.

Josh had been lucky enough to get a job with
Northumbria County Council as an archaeologist and
Joanne worked for a legal firm in the adjoining market
town of Hexham. Their small stone cottage backed on
to the river Tyne and the garden, steeply terraced, ran
down to the softly flowing water. The house rang with
laughter and love, and anticipation of a happy event.

At first Rebecca almost resented the happiness her
friends shared. Each morning she pulled herself out of
bed, usually after a sleepless night or worse. When she
slept her dreams were full of Benedict, and the touch of
his hands, the warmth of his lips were so real; and then
she would wake, her body flushed and wanting, and
know it was all a dream. Sadly that was all her relationship with Benedict had ever been.

But gradually the peace and beauty of her surroundings began to soothe her bruised heart. She drove
all over the county, parking her car at various spots along
the route of Hadrian's Wall and walking for hours. She

visited Housesteads, the Roman fort, and from there walked miles along the top of the wall.

There was something remarkably levelling about standing on a wall that was thousands of years old and thinking of the men, beginning with the Roman legions, who had spent centuries guarding this wild landscape. Finally she could see her actions of the last few months in perspective. So she had an unfortunate love-affair. So what? In the space and timeless beauty of the Northumbrian landscape, she began to realise that life was too short to dwell on past mistakes. Man's span on earth was all too brief in the greater scheme of things, and she would only be compounding her foolish behaviour if she allowed a few weeks with Benedict Maxwell to overshadow her whole life.

By the time Rebecca was once more on the road back to Oxford she had regained some peace of mind and some of her confidence. The bitterness she felt towards Benedict would probably always be with her. But she was lucky. She had good friends and an interesting career to look forward to, and in time perhaps she would find the perfect partner...

The red painted door was so familiar. Rebecca raised her hand to knock, but before she got the chance the door was flung open, and she was clasped in a warm embrace.

'Rebecca! It's good to see you,' Mary cried, and, holding her arm, led her into the living-room. 'But I have some rather bad news.'

'Jonathan? He is all right?'

'Yes, he's fine, getting fatter by the minute.' Mary turned worried eyes on her young friend. 'But that dumb ox of a husband of mine has done something so stupid, I could throttle him.'

'Rupert?' Rebecca queried, sinking gracefully on to the shabby sofa. She knew the man was a bit absent-minded but she could not see him doing anything to hurt his family deliberately. 'What has he done?'

'Benedict Maxwell rang yesterday.'

Rebecca swallowed hard, fighting down her instant reaction to the sound of his name, and, with a lightness she did not feel, she said offhandedly, 'So?'

'He rang to confirm that he was still standing as a godfather to Jonathan and he'll be down tomorrow for the christening. Rupert, fool that he is, said, "Yes, fine," and has only seen fit to tell me half an hour ago. I'm sorry, love. I've tried to get in touch with Benedict, but so far no joy.'

'Is that all?' Rebecca laughed lightly, wanting to save her friend's obvious embarrassment. But her insides churned sickeningly. She had not thought she would have to face Benedict again, and certainly not tomorrow. The gall of the man was fantastic. Mary had asked them both to be godparents, but that was when she had thought they were engaged. The least he could have done, given the circumstnces, was bow out gracefully. He was just doing this to torment her.

'Rebecca, I know you said it was a mutual decision for the two of you to part, but, my dear, I have known you for four years, and I know you're hurting. If there is any way I can stop Benedict coming, I will.'

'Don't bother, Mary, I'll be all right, honestly.' But she could not hide the tremor in her voice. Coming back to this house had awakened memories she had tried so hard to forget.

Mary walked over and sat down next to her on the sofa. Rebecca made no protest as Mary gathered her hands in hers. 'Sometimes it's better to talk, love.'

Whether it was the touch of human warmth, the softness of Mary's voice or just weeks of bottling up the truth, Rebecca did not know. But for the next fifteen minutes she found herself confiding everything that had happened between herself and Benedict and the story of Gordon.

'You poor child,' Mary crooned, sliding an arm around her shoulders.

For a moment Rebecca allowed herself to wallow in the comfort of the other woman's sympathy, then, with a deep sigh, she straightened. 'I'm OK now, Mary. My holiday has helped me put things in perspective, and you've nothing to worry about tomorrow. I'll be fine at the christening.'

'I don't give a fig about that . . . Well, I do. But I can't believe Ben could be so thoroughly rotten, though I suppose in a way I'm not surprised. True, I knew him as a boy at college, but he was very reserved then and somehow, meeting him fourteen years later, I sensed a hardness about him; but, after what had happened to him, I thought, What can one expect from someone who has spent years cut off from civilisation? But to deliberately set out to hurt you . . . Words fail me.'

'My sentiments exactly, Mary. And now, if you don't mind, I think I'll go to bed. We have a busy day ahead of us tomorrow.'

It was another beautiful summer day; the sun beat down from an azure sky. Rebecca had spent all morning helping in the kitchen, running back and forward to the back garden, where the buffet was to be held, setting up trestle-tables, anything she could find to keep herself busy. She didn't want to think about her forthcoming meeting with Benedict.

Finally Mary hustled her off upstairs to get ready for church. 'One hour exactly. Get ready!'

Rebecca watched from the bedroom window as the cars pulled up in the street outside. She said a silent prayer of thanks. Rupert and Mary's parents had arrived first, so at least now when Benedict turned up she would not be left on her own to entertain him, while Mary got the baby ready for the short journey to the church.

She smoothed the slim pink silk skirt over her slender hips—too slender... The last and only time she had worn the outfit was for her first dinner date with Benedict. Well, it was stupid to be sentimental about clothes, she told herself firmly, and defiantly buttoned the jacket.

Only she had lost a bit of weight in the past few weeks and where once the small, fitted short-sleeved jacket had fastened snugly around her waist there was now room to spare, and the skirt no longer clung to her hips. Still, it wasn't too noticeable. Worriedly she chewed her bottom lip; if her suspicion was correct loss of weight would very soon not be a problem. With one last glance in the dressing-table mirror, she patted her neatly curled chignon and left the room.

With furtive glances at her wristwatch she carried the tray of drinks around the living-room, Rupert's booming voice, full of happiness, almost concealing the sound of the doorbell. Fortunately his mother-in-law jumped up and answered it. It could only be Benedict. Tom and Rose Wiltshire, the other godparents, had already arrived.

Rebecca felt the hairs on the back of her neck stand on end, her heart missed a beat, and she berated herself for being so stupid. Taking a deep breath and slowly exhaling, she turned around and not by a flicker of an eyelid did she betray her nervous tension as she coolly walked across the room and offered the latest arrival a drink.

'Whisky or sherry, Mr Maxwell?' she proferred, avoiding his eyes. 'Help yourself.'

'Hello, Rebecca.' Her violet eyes followed the progress of his large, tanned hand as he reached out, his long fingers curving around the chubby thickness of a crystal glass. 'A whisky will do fine—and Benedict, please.'

She could not tear her gaze away from the light smattering of black hairs at his wrist, the edge of his immaculate white silk shirt peeking beneath the grey silk sleeve of his jacket. She followed his hand as he raised the glass to his mouth, and quite unconsciously the tip of her tongue flicked out and licked her dry lips, as for a moment she remembered the touch of his sensuous mouth on her own.

'Surely after the intimacy we have shared you can't insist on calling me Mr Maxwell.'

His words stabbed her like a knife. She raised her eyes to his, and for a moment it was as though they were the only two people in the room. His golden gaze was strangely intent, no trace of the triumph she had expected evident there.

'You wore that outfit on our first date. You looked beautiful then, and you look even more beautiful now.'

He had the nerve to remind her. He was actually flirting with her. She wanted to smack his handsome face, she was so mad, but instead she replied calmly, 'Did I? I don't remember.'

'You do. But I suppose your denial was to be expected.' His dark head inclined towards her. 'Are you all right, Rebecca?'

Was she all right? Good God, if only he knew! It had been a month since their last meeting, and she had spent the last two weeks worrying. She was almost sure she was pregnant. She was clinging to the forlorn hope that emotional upheaval had disturbed her monthly cycle, but the nausea she had suffered that very morning led her to suspect the worst. But there was no way on earth she would tell this man...

'I'm fine, thank you,' she bit out. 'Excuse me, I have to attend to the guests.' She could not get away quick enough.

'Rebecca, wait.'

'Ah, Becky, you darling, give me a drink quick and let's get this show on the road before baby Jonathan here decides to have another screaming fit.'

Rebecca expelled a sigh of relief at Mary's timely intervention, and in the general exodus for the cars to the church she managed to avoid Benedict.

Standing by the font of the old church with Benedict beside her, his sleeve brushing her shoulder, she could not help but be aware of him. She cast him a sidelong glance. He looked devilishly attractive, his dark hair, slightly longer, now curved the collar of his perfectly tailored jacket. He moved slightly and his muscular thigh rested against her; she jerked away as though she had been electrocuted, and barely managed to respond to the minister. Luckily no one seemed to have noticed her confusion.

Except Benedict. He turned towards her, his dark eyes lit with amusement. 'We're in a church, Rebecca, you're perfectly safe... For now.'

The whispered words ignited her anger but there was nothing she could do about it; nevertheless it took all her self-control to prevent herself giving him a hefty kick in the shin. The conceited swine.

Back at the house Rebecca tried to avoid Benedict, but everywhere she moved he seemed to appear at her elbow. She fixed a smile on her face and talked vivaciously to everyone but him.

'I'll get you alone in the end, Rebecca,' he drawled softly, close to her ear.

Over my dead body, she thought, bitterly moving away, and breathing a sigh of relief as Fiona Grieves arrived with the Chancellor and his wife. Fiona made a bee-line for Benedict, linking her arm with his, and gazing adoringly at him.

Rebecca told herself she didn't care, the other woman was welcome to him, but her gaze kept straying to where he stood. A powerful, dynamic man, he drew people to him by the sheer force of his presence. He looked up and their eyes met. Benedict winked...

Amazement was quickly followed by disgust with herself and she lowered her gaze. She took a deep breath; it was almost over, and she had survived. But she could not relax, her nerves were tied in knots.

Perhaps indoors, away from the crowd, might give her some measure of relief, she thought as she strode into the living-room. The christening presents were laid out neatly on a table and idly she read the accompanying cards, smiling at 'Go for the set' beside a silver napkin-ring.

'If I were in your shoes I wouldn't be smiling.'

Fiona! How had she managed to tear herself away from Benedict? Rebecca thought cattily, when out of the corner of her eye, through the open door, she saw Mary ushering the man into the study across the hall.

'Oh, I don't know; I think the party is going rather well,' she replied, politely ignoring the other woman's innuendo.

'Come off it, Rebecca. You had the greatest catch of the decade and let him slip away.'

'An anthropologist can hardly be called the greatest catch of the decade. A multi-millionaire, maybe,' she opined mockingly, wishing Fiona would shut up.

'You don't know. I honestly believe you don't know.' The red-haired head was thrown back and she laughed.

The high, false sound grated on Rebecca's taut nerves and no way was she going to ask the question Fiona was evidently waiting for.

'My dear, Benedict Maxwell is a millionaire and more. Surely you have heard of M and M, the Anglo-French electronics firm?' Fiona waited and when Rebecca still stared blankly at her she continued, 'Montaine and Maxwell. The whole story was on the Jeff Kates show on television a couple of weeks ago. He interviewed Benedict and made him furious by suggesting he wasn't a genuine anthropologist and his discovery of the tribe and everything was all pure luck.'

'That's ridiculous.' Why Rebecca was defending Benedict's academic achievements, she had no idea.

'You know what they say. Money comes to money, fame to fame and all that. Apparently Benedict was on a two-year sabbatical from the family firm. When he was presumed dead, his uncle, Gerard Montaine, ran the company virtually on his own. But now Benedict is back and chairman of the board.'

Rebecca stared open-mouthed at Fiona. M and M was Benedict's. She had heard of it—anyone who ever read the business pages had. They had done a vast amount of the electronics work on the Channel Tunnel. Of course. Gordon had told her his mother was French. Benedict's mother... Good God! She had been an even bigger idiot than she knew.

'Rebecca, I want a word with you.' Steely fingers grabbed her arm and she found herself looking up into the darkly flushed face of Benedict. 'Alone,' he snarled, anger in every inch of him.

Something or someone had evidently rubbed the great man the wrong way; the air crackled with tension. But Rebecca had no intention of allowing herself to be used as the scapegoat. He had done that to her once already, never again...

'Benedict, darling, I thought you were never coming back,' Fiona's high-pitched whine intruded.

'Get lost, Fiona, I want to talk to my ex-fiancée.'

Rebecca almost felt sorry for the other girl; her beautifully made-up face turned scarlet and, with a haughty toss of her head, she walked out of the room.

'That was rather brutal, but true to form,' Rebecca observed coolly. Benedict's hand on her arm tightened. 'Let go of me,' she snapped.

'After we have had our little talk you can go to hell, but first I want an explanation.'

One quick glance at his dark face and she allowed him to lead her across the hall and into the study. She would never forgive herself if he caused a scene at the christening. She would not allow this man to spoil one of the happiest days of Mary's life.

Benedict was controlling his temper by a thread. It was evident in every line of his body, the tight, hard mouth, and the glitter of rage in his golden eyes. What had upset him, she could not imagine, but a shiver of fear snaked down her spine as the study door was slammed shut behind her.

'Now, Rebecca, just what the hell have you been telling Mary? I have never been so insulted in my life. Not five minutes ago I was raked over the coals for my despicable behaviour, by a woman I have known for years. Mary was sorry—if she could have contacted me, I would have not been needed as a godfather to her son. And it's all your doing.'

Rebecca groaned, she should have guessed. Mary was staunchly loyal, and very outspoken. The glimpse earlier of Mary and Benedict, entering this room, suddenly made sense.

'Why such outrage, Benedict? Surely it was no more than you expected?' She forced herself to stay calm,

though inside she was sick with misery. It had never occurred to her that Mary would tackle Benedict...

'I didn't expect to be virtually accused of rape,' he
snarled, and, his hands closing on her slender shoulders,
he hauled her tight against his huge, taut body. His dark
head swooped, and before she could react his mouth
savaged hers in a brutal kiss, his fingers tangling in the
mass of her black hair, with one tug dismantling the
smooth chignon.

Rebecca flinched, her hair cascading around her
shoulders. Then inexplicably the kiss gentled and he
murmured husky words against her mouth. To her shame
she sighed a soft sound of surrender. He straightened
up, and held her at arm's length, his glittering gaze intent
upon the pink, swollen curve of her mouth, the tell-tale
flush on her lovely face.

'If Mary could see you now she would know you for
the liar you are. Seduced you for revenge—what a joke!
You couldn't keep your hands off me,' he said scathingly.

It was worse than Rebecca had thought. Not only had
Mary confronted him about the break-up, but she had
obviously added her own suspicions about Rebecca's reaction to his lovemaking.

'I...I didn't lie to Mary. She is my friend, and—and
I told her the truth.' She stuttered over the words. Just
when she thought she had begun to get her life in order,
it was starting all over again. Benedict...was she never
to be free of him...?

'Your version—Gordon isn't around to deny it.'

She thrust the pain away at the mention of his half-
brother, and, very composed because she was keeping a
tight rein on her fast-rising temper, she said, 'Gordon
would have agreed with me. He was a wonderful, caring
young man. Something you would know nothing about.'

'By God, woman, you're truly remarkable! I look in
those wide, innocent violet eyes, and even I could be

fooled for a second. But I know just how destructive
you can be. Poor Mary is as deceived by you as Gordon
was. I've known the woman since we were teenagers,
and in four short years you twine yourself around her
affections so much so, you tell her what a big, bad ogre
I am, and years of friendship are destroyed.' She
stumbled backwards as Benedict thrust her away from
him. 'You disgust me!' he snorted contemptuously.

Rebecca looked at him slowly through her thick lashes.
He was standing motionless, arrogant contempt in every
line of his hard body.

'What, no come-back, Rebecca?' He drawled her
name as if it were an insult.

It was the last straw for Rebecca, and, straightening,
she proudly raised her head, while with one hand she
brushed her tangled mass of night-black hair from her
face. 'You're pathetic, Benedict. My father once told me
everyone is responsible for his or her own actions, but
you—you're a coward and a cheat.'

'I've never hit a woman, but you could well be the
first,' Benedict growled, taking a step towards her.

'It wouldn't surprise me. Nothing you do could surprise me any more. I've finally got your number, Mr
Maxwell. You needed a scapegoat to assuage your own
guilt... Mary, the friend who has only had a couple of
cards off you in donkey's years, told me you were never
there for your mother. Poor Gordon, as you like to call
him, was a hundred times better a son. Where were you
when your family needed you? Swanning around in
Brazil.'

Rebecca saw the colour leave his face, his lips tightened to a thin line edged in white as he struggled to
control his fury, but nothing could stop her. She wanted
to hurt him as he had hurt her.

'Gordon told me he was spending the holiday with his
mother because she needed him... He was that kind of

young man. Unselfish. But then, how would you know, Benedict? You barely knew the boy.'

Benedict flinched, and she knew she had hit a nerve, but she didn't care. Nothing could stop her now.

'He told me his mother was distraught at losing her husband, and at your presumed death. He missed his father but, as he had rarely seen you, it didn't bother him as much. So if you want to lay blame anywhere, try laying it on yourself, you selfish bastard. And, before you call me a liar again, I suggest you read the autopsy report on Gordon. For a man who is supposed to be a scientist, your research is sadly lacking.'

She stalked across to the door and Benedict made no move to stop her. She turned, with her hand on the door-knob, and as a parting shot she added spitefully, 'Maybe that television chappy was right, Mr Multi-Millionaire. Your success in the Amazon *was* luck...' Rebecca flounced out of the study without a backward glance, she was so furious.

If she had stayed she would have seen Benedict Maxwell collapse in a chair and bury his head in his hands...

CHAPTER FIVE

'*MERCI*.' Rebecca picked up the cup of coffee the waiter had placed on the table, took a sip, and sank a few inches lower in the chair. A soft sigh of contentment escaped her. No one made coffee like the French. For the first time in three days she was alone and at peace.

The marina at Royan sparkled in the June sun, the sailing boats lying low in the water, their tall masts creaking and jingling in the strong breeze, the sound blending melodiously with the chattering voices of the locals enjoying the Sunday holiday.

Her attention was caught by a young boy crying as his ice-cream plopped on the pavement, and she was achingly reminded of her own son Daniel. It was the first time she had left him with Joanne and Josh, and she missed him dreadfully. But as a single parent she had to look after her career.

Her gaze strayed to a large yacht navigating the entrance to the harbour. A gleaming white cruiser, it was too big for the narrow berth of the marina, and tracked the harbour wall to dock at the open wharf. A tall, dark-headed man appeared on deck. He jumped lightly to the shore, his tanned body gleaming in the afternoon sun. Rebecca could not see his face, but there was something oddly familiar about him, the lithe way he moved, but before she could pursue the thought the peaceful setting was shattered by the strident cry of a young girl running towards the café.

'Mrs Blacket-Green . . . Mrs Blacket-Green!'

Rebecca groaned, and looked up as the girl stopped in front of her. 'What's wrong, Dolores?' She eyed the well-developed sixteen-year-old, and frowned at the apology for a bikini she was wearing. 'And didn't I tell all you girls not to leave the beach without some clothes on?'

'Yes, miss. But please, miss, you have to come quick. Dodger persuaded Mr Humphrey to go out on a hobby cat and now they're in real trouble.'

Rebecca jumped to her feet. Extracting a few francs from the pocket of her trousers, she dropped them on the table, and set off at a run down the hill towards the beach. The large, dark man standing on the wharf was forgotten. She never noticed him turn to watch them, or the arrested expression on his rugged face.

The school trip to France had started off badly. On Friday, when they left England, Miss Smythe, her co-driver, had jammed her hand in the door of the minibus, and, as her other colleague, Mr Humphrey, didn't drive, Rebecca was left with the task, along with much of the responsibility for looking after a group of sixteen-year-old schoolchildren.

Oh, God! What damn fool thing had Humphrey done now? Rebecca asked herself, as she reached the beach. Miss Smythe was at the villa, preparing the evening meal, but Rebecca had felt sure Humphrey could manage on his own for a few minutes. Looking across the water, obviously she had been wrong. Travelling fast towards the entrance of the Gironde estuary and the Atlantic beyond was a hobby cat, the wind full in a large white sail and two figures getting smaller by the second clinging to the canvas deck.

'Dolores, get the rest of the pupils, and meet me at the shoreline,' she ordered, dashing across the sand. Then, to Rebecca's immense relief, she realised that the antics of the two on the cat had been spotted. Three lifeguards shot past her, and as she watched they jumped into a motorised dinghy, and in minutes reached the sailboat and fastened a line to it.

Rebecca sighed with relief as the boat was towed to the shore. With her fast-beating heart returning to normal, she walked to the water's edge, gathering up her charges as she went. There were nine—five boys and four girls, with the iniquitous Dodger, Mr Humphrey, Miss Smythe and herself making up the party of thirteen! Some omen...

She watched, a worried frown creasing her face, as the men stepped ashore, while the rest of her pupils cheered. Once she had assured herself no harm had come to the would-be sailors, her relief gave way to anger.

'Right, you lot. Sit down! Not you, Mr Humphrey—perhaps you could go and get the sports gear while I talk to the children.' She eyed him with exasperation. A tall, ginger-haired, bespectacled young man, in the four years Rebecca had taught at the large comprehensive school in one of the poorer areas of London, Mr Humphrey had definitely proved himself the most unlikely man to control the street-smart kids.

'Silence!' she shouted, viewing the motley collection with jaundiced eyes until she found the culprit. 'Right, Dodger, perhaps you would care to explain your behaviour.'

'I fancied a sail, miss. We are on holiday.'

Three days and already she was a nervous wreck. 'Let me tell you. All of you. Unless you smarten your ideas up, I will drive the bus back home tomorrow.' She was totally unaware of the startling picture she presented. A tiny, beautifully shaped woman, with short black curly hair, dressed in cut-offs, a skimpy black Lycra boob-tube, and a pair of battered Reeboks on her dainty feet... haranguing a group of teenagers all bigger than her.

'This trip started with an accident and but for the life-
guard today would have ended in catastrophe. How you
dared pretend you could sail, Dodger——' her eyes fixed
on the youth responsible for the trouble '—when I know
the nearest you have been to sailing is a rowing boat on
the Serpentine in Hyde Park, is completely beyond me.
An——'

Loud masculine laughter stopped her and, unsus-
pecting, she looked around. The catastrophe had happened after all. Benedict Maxwell. She recognised him
immediately, her heart slamming against her ribcage in
shock. Five years since their last meeting, and he had
laughed then, she recalled, all the old bitterness returning, but with it a sense of pride. He could not hurt
her now.

'Rebecca, Rebecca,' he spluttered between gales of
laughter, 'you achieved your ambition, I see.' His golden
eyes lit with amsuement, flashed around the group.
'Where do you teach? At a school for delinquents?'

He was standing a few feet away, naked except for
brief khaki shorts, his wide shoulders shaking with mirth.
Pointedly she turned her back on the laughing man, not
deigning to answer him, and carried on in a firm voice,
'I want you, Dodger and Thompkins, to pick two teams
and set up a game of football. Hopefully that will keep
you out of trouble for an hour or two.'

'Hey, miss, the bloke is still there. Why don't you
speak to him?' Dolores piped up. 'He's not bad for an
old guy.'

Rebecca didn't want to speak to Benedict, she didn't
even want to acknowledge his existence, but her lips
twitched. 'Old guy.' He would love that...

'This old guy is perfectly capable of speaking for
himself. Why don't you children jump to it and do as
your teacher said? Football. Now.'

Rebecca had not realised Benedict was so close. A large hand curved over her shoulder, and she flinched at the impact on her smooth flesh. With a quick shrug she stepped away. 'I am perfectly able to look after my pupils. I don't need your assistance.'

'Forgive me, Rebecca.' Amusement still quirked his sensuous lips, but his dark gaze was intent and oddly serious on her flushed face. For a second she had the impression he was asking more than his words implied. But she was quickly disabused of the notion when he added mockingly, 'but you look as if you need all the help you can get.'

'You're the last man on earth I would ask if I did,' she spat. What perverse twist of fate had brought this man to this beach in the south-west of France, on the very day she had arrived? Rebecca asked herself bitterly. She had hoped never to see Benedict again, and after five years thought she had succeeded.

'That's better, Rebecca. It's good to see you're the same little firecracker I knew.' His lips parted over gleaming white teeth in a wolfish smile. 'And loved,' he added silkily.

Liar. He had never loved her, and she had no intention of bandying words with the man. A scream was a welcome diversion and she turned her attention to the ball game. 'You were offside, Dolores,' she cried, ending what looked like becoming an argument, before calling to her colleague, 'Mr Humphrey, I'll take over. I think you've had enough sun for one day.' The action might stop her legs trembling . . .

'Not so fast, Rebecca.' A big hand closed around her upper arm.

She glanced up at Benedict. He was standing much too close; she could feel the heat, the power coming from his muscled body, his glittering gaze commanding her attention.

'I want to talk to you, I want to explain. I want you
to give me a chance,' he declared hardily.

Five years rolled back, and for a second she was once
again the besotted fool. She shivered. She had been
wrong earlier. This man could hurt her again. If he ever
discovered her secret...

'Still the same Benedict: "I want".' A muscle tensed
along his square jaw was the only visible sign of his rising
temper. 'Well, you will just have to want. It will be a
new experience for you, I'm sure,' she said with cold
cynicism. 'And get your hand off me.'

'You win for now,' he said quietly, setting her free,
as Mr Humphrey walked towards them. 'I can see this
isn't the right time, Rebecca. Will you have dinner with
me tonight?'

'No. I will not,' she said bluntly, and she caught the
predatory flash in his tiger eyes an instant before Mr
Humphrey joined them. Saved, she thought, deliberately turning her attention on Humphrey.

'Thanks, Rebecca. I am starting to burn.' The young
man grimaced. 'See you later.' And with a wave he loped
off down the beach.

In her peripheral vision she picked up what looked
like the start of another argument. She wanted to ignore
Benedict but her innate good manners forced her to turn
back to him. 'Goodbye, Mr Ma——'

'Not so fast.' He stepped closer, his size, the well-
muscled contours of his big, near-naked body disturb-
ingly intimidating. 'Why, Rebecca?' One dark brow
raised in enquiry. 'What are you afraid of?'

If only he knew... A thread of caution warned her
to be careful. Her violet eyes wide, and she hoped
innocent, lifted to his. 'Snakes, maybe,' she said mus-
ingly, 'but certainly not you.' She watched him stiffen,
his face tight as the meaning of her words sank in. 'You
will have to excuse me. My pupils need me.'

And, swinging around, she ran across the makeshift
pitch. She felt his eyes burning into her back, but forced
herself to ignore his brooding presence on the sidelines.
She concentrated all her attention on the game.

She heaved a deep sigh of relief when, out of the corner
of her eye, she saw Benedict turn and walk back up to
the road. Thank God! He had gone...

Midnight and the house was finally quiet. It had been
a long day. They had spent two days in Paris, left early
that morning and driven down to Royan, arriving at
lunchtime, and Rebecca was exhausted. The house they
were staying in was a lovely old building on the roadside,
overlooking the beach. It belonged to Miss Smythe; she
had bought it for a song a few years ago for her re-
tirement. She intended eventually to turn it into a holiday
centre for students with limited funds. It had three large
reception-rooms, four bedrooms on the first floor plus
bathroom, and another four attic rooms and bathroom.
The boys had opted for the attics and the girls had the
first floor.

Wearily Rebecca made her way upstairs and into her
room, switching off the lights as she went. She shrugged
off her clothes and climbed into bed, too tired to think.
But an hour later she was still awake. She tried to tell
herself it was the heat, but she knew she was lying.
Benedict Maxwell was the sole cause of her insomnia.

Her mind went back to their last meeting five years
ago. After storming out of the study she had spent ten
minutes tidying herself up and pride alone had forced
her to return to the christening party.

Benedict had been politely making his goodbyes, his
anger at Rebecca held firmly in check. When he'd spotted
her coming downstairs, he had strolled up to her and
declared loudly, 'It was wonderful seeing you again,

darling, and I'm sure we will always be good friends.'
Then he'd had the audacity to kiss her.

She had been jumping with anger, too furious to
speak, and his laughter echoed in her head long after he
had left. The next day she had moved to Nottingham,
renting one room while she completed her teacher-
training course.

The days were bearable with lectures to occupy her
mind, but at night, alone, she cried and cried. Often the
dawn found her awake and hurting.

She visited Oxord once more for Rupert and Mary's
farewell party in October, and on her return to
Nottingham the full folly of her actions was brought
home to her. She finally visited the doctor and her preg-
nancy was confirmed.

She exchanged her bedsit for a two-roomed apartment,
and, spending Christmas with Joanne and Josh, she had
confided in them. They had been a tower of strength for
her. Daniel was born in the Easter break and Joanne
had stayed with Rebecca for over a month.

It had all worked out very well. Rebecca took her final
exams and passed with flying colours. She applied for
a teaching post in a London school, and was immediately accepted, then spent the rest of the summer with
her new baby, and house-hunting.

Rebecca flung her legs over the bed and walked across
to the window. Her eyes roamed over the wide beach to
the sea beyond, the waves gently lapping the shore like
a lover's caress, a full moon gilding the scene in silver
glow. She was filled with doubt, and it was Benedict
Maxwell's fault... Had she done the right thing? yes,
of course, she told herself, her eyes lifting to the star-
studded night sky, as if by some miracle the heavens
would confirm the correctness of her decision.

She shivered. A chance meeting and, if she wasn't
careful, her cosy life could be badly disrupted.

*   *   *

'I brought a friend, is that OK?'

Rebecca jumped, dropping the sausage she had been trying to fork off the barbecue. 'Damn!' she swore under her breath and slowly turned to face the couple strolling across the garden. Dolores, with Benedict Maxwell in tow, was grinning all over her young face, the rest of the group behind them.

'We met your friend and invited him to lunch.'

'I hope you don't mind?' Benedict came towards her, his golden gaze roaming over her scantily clad body with sensual appreciation.

Rebecca shivered inwardly, and wished she had dressed with more care—brief shorts and a bikini-top were no defence against Benedict's studied appraisal. But even more worrying to her peace of mind was, what was he doing here? Miss Smythe had taken the children to explore the town. How Dolores had ended up with Benedict, she couldn't imagine.

Her eyes skated over his large frame. He was wearing a black sleeveless sweatshirt that outlined the musculature of his chest, beige chinos hugged his hips, a pair of Gucci loafers on his feet—the overall impression all virile male.

'Yesterday I was mad you had cut your hair; I remember it spread on my pillow,' he said softly. 'But now I like it,' Then he ran one large hand through her short black curly hair.

She flinched beneath his casual caress, and the memory his words invoked, and hit out at him scathingly, 'I should have thought even you would have more sense than to chat up young teenagers.'

'Don't be stupid, Rebecca. You must know the only reason I spoke to Dolores was to find you.'

She believed him. The trouble was, she had not wanted him to find her again. He was a dangerous man, and she had far too much to lose... She turned wary, hostile eyes to his, about to tell him to get lost, when Miss Smythe cut in, 'Isn't it lucky we met your old friend Mr Maxwell? Fancy your father being one of his lecturers at university! What a small world it is. I was telling him about my little accident——' she held her bandaged hand before her '—and guess what?'

The flash of triumph in Benedict's eyes was enough to tell Rebecca that she was not going to like the answer.

'His yacht is here in the harbour for a few days, while some minor repairs are carried out. So he has kindly offered to help with the driving for a couple of days. Also the children are going for a trip on his boat on Thursday. Isn't that great?'

Stifling a groan—it was worse than she thought— Rebecca said firmly, 'Really, I don't think we can impose on Mr Maxwell like that.'

'Nonsense, Rebecca, it's my privilege,' Benedict drawled mockingly. 'What are friends for?'

She shot him a fulminating look; it was obvious he had spent the last hour winning the confidence of her two colleagues and the children. She could just imagine their faces if she told them the truth. He had seduced her and given her a child...Daniel. The thought of her son cooled her anger; she had to be careful. One slip and Benedict might find out more than she wanted him to know. Screaming her hatred of him was a non-starter. Much better to play him at his own game. Pretend to be friends, and in a few days' time she need never see him again.

'Well, if you're sure it won't be too much trouble?' she queried lightly, amazed at her own acting ability. 'Your help with the driving would be much appreciated.' The kids would drive him mad in half a day and it would serve the swine right, she thought gleefully.

'It will be my pleasure, Rebecca.'

Little did he know... She had no doubt his experience was zilch. He was in for a rude awakening. Confidently she turned to the large trestle-table with long benches running either side and began setting out the food.

Rebecca was not quite so confident when she realised the only place left to sit was at the end of the bench next to Benedict, and when his hard thigh brushed her naked leg she quickly edged away.

'Nervous, Rebecca? There's no need. Have a drink,' he drawled softly, and, picking up the large bottle of cheap wine, he leant over her and filled the beaker beside her on the table. 'It should be champagne to celebrate our reunion.'

His throatily voiced comment was a teasing breath across her cheek, his golden eyes glittered wickedly down at her, and in that instant she knew she was not immune to his charm and never would be.

'Hardly a reunion,' she said carefully.

A lazy smile curved his hard mouth. 'Oh, but yes, Rebecca, and I'm hoping for a lot more,' he drawled, his gaze dropping from her lovely face to her full breasts, arousing an unwanted shiver of awareness inside her. 'I'm looking forward to tomorrow and accompanying you to Cognac. Wednesday is a nature trail, I believe, and Thursday we go sailing.'

'There's no need,' she snapped, forgetting her early conviction to beat him at his own game.

'Oh, but I think you do need me, Rebecca.'

She flushed and looked away. She didn't need him, she didn't need any man, she told herself sternly.

'To help with the children, of course. Dolores tells me you're here until Friday, so perhaps we could have that dinner after all,' he said blandly.

Stupid, stupid, stupid, Rebecca castigated herself. Of course Benedict had not meant she needed him personally. 'Dolores has a big mouth,' she muttered.

'Now, now, Rebecca; is that any way to talk about your pupils?' he admonished with a chuckle.

She ignored him and savagely speared the sausage on her plate, wishing it was Benedict's face. As for Dolores... She would have to have words with that girl. God knew what else she might tell him. It was a short step from gossiping about Rebecca's school duties to her personal life, and she could not allow that to happen. Lifting the plastic beaker to her lips, she took a long swallow of wine in an attempt to steady her nerves. Then, replacing it on the picnic table, she munched on a sausage. When she finally had enough control to raise her head, and tune into the conversation, to her horror she saw that Benedict was arranging with Miss Smythe and Mr Humphrey for him to take her out to dinner on Wednesday evening.

'No, really,' she cut in. 'I couldn't leave you two on your own with the children.'

'Rubbish, Rebecca, you'll be doing most of the work the next couple of days, of course you must have a night out with your old friend. I won't hear otherwise,' Miss Smythe insisted.

Rebecca's violet eyes flashed fire at the man beside her. His smug, self-satisfied grin, and the triumph in his eyes, made her clench her teeth to prevent herself cursing out loud. Benedict Maxwell was an expert at manipulating circumstances and people to suit himself. If he was determined to spend the next couple of days with their party, and to get Rebecca alone, he must have some ulterior motive for it. With a terrific effort of will she retained her self-control. It would be more to her advantage to expend her energies on trying to find out exactly what he was up to...

She tilted her head to one side, and for the first time since meeting him again she really studied him. He was thinner, the lines bracketing his mouth much deeper, the once-black hair now streaked with grey. He looked a lot older than she remembered; still, he was almost forty. But it wasn't the signs of age that made him look different—the hard character of the man was etched into his rugged features. Or perhaps it was because she no longer saw him through a rosy haze of love; her vision had cleared, and she saw him for what he was: a dangerous man...

'So will I do?' Benedict asked drily. 'You're looking at me as though you've never seen me before.'

An embarrassing tide of colour swept up her throat and she could have kicked herself for being caught staring. Instead, picking her words with care, she replied, 'Five years is a long time, I don't know you; but from what I remember of you——' she deftly brought the subject back to the present '—I find it difficult to believe you would willingly spend time with a group of schoolchildren. I would have thought the Riviera was more your style.'

'How would you know my style, Rebecca? After you broke off our engagement you refused to even acknowledge my existence,' he said with bitter cynicism.

She broke off their engagement? 'Hardly surprising,' she snorted inelegantly. Who was he trying to kid? Had the man lost his memory?

'I know I was wrong, but I wrote and explained, apologised. I hoped you would reply, but I understood and accepted it when you didn't. But surely after five years you can forgive me?' he demanded, frustration evident in his voice.

He had lost her. Benedict had never written to her in his life.

'I want to be your friend, Rebecca—lay the ghost of the past once and for all. Yesterday, when I saw you at the harbour, I couldn't believe my luck. My one thought was at last I had a chance to put things right between us. A letter is never really satisfactory.' His deep voice was compelling but Rebecca could not believe what she was hearing.

Thankfully Miss Smythe interrupted the low conversation with, 'Well, if you all help to clean up, the rest of the afternoon can be spent on the beach.'

Benedict looked around as though he had forgotten there were other people present, and swore under his breath. He glanced back at Rebecca.

'We will talk, and that's a promise.' The threat in his tone was unmistakable and, not waiting for her reply, he got to his feet. With all the charm at his disposal he regretfully took his leave—business to attend to. With one last penetrating look at Rebecca, he added, 'Miss Smythe tells me we leave at nine in the morning. I'll see you then.'

'Yes, fine, goodbye,' she gritted, galled to have to agree, but she had no option.

For the rest of the afternoon Rebecca kept a sketchy eye on her pupils, while going over and over in her mind everything that had happened since yesterday afternoon and the reappearance of Benedict Maxwell in her life.

Could she have handled the situation any differently? she asked herself a hundred times over. The answer was always no. With his easy charm he had completely captivated Miss Smythe, and she was the senior teacher. Rebecca was obliged to go along with what her colleague suggested. Cutting Benedict dead, or allowing her bitterness to show, would serve no purpose. He would probably see it as a challenge and be even more persistent or, worse, suspicious. An inquisitive Benedict was the last thing she needed. Yes. She had done the right thing. The next few days would be hard, but then back to London and safety.

Later, after dinner, she made a quick telephone call to Josh and Joanne in Corbridge and spent a happy five minutes talking to Daniel. He was having a great time with young Amy to play with, and did not appear to miss her in the least. Afterwards she wandered outside, unable to settle. Benedict's reappearance had disturbed her more than she wanted to admit. Daniel was the image of him; she had not quite realised how very alike they were until today, and the thought was oddly disturbing...

Sitting in the front passenger-seat of the minibus, she cast a sidelong glance at the driver. Benedict looked positively brimming with health and vitality, his rugged features somehow more relaxed. She couldn't see the expression in his eyes as he was wearing dark glasses, but, by the upward curve of his lips, he was a man content with the world.

Rebecca was loath to admit it, but it was a relief to have someone else drive. She had not relished the thought of doing it all herself.

'Why the frown, Rebecca?' The softly voiced question caught her unawares. 'Is it such a hardship to be in my company?

Her full lips curved up in a smile. 'No, nothing like that; in fact I was just thinking how lucky we are to have you along. I like driving, but it's good to have a break,' she replied truthfully.

'I'm sorry Miss Smythe hurt her hand, but her loss is my gain, so I'm not complaining.' He turned his attention back to the road, adding wryly, 'Except about the dilapidated state of this vehicle. It amazes me you managed to drive it from England.'

'It's perfectly all right, only a bit old; it needs gentling along, that's all,' she defended.

He shot her a cheeky grin. 'Like me.'

She turned and looked out of the window, warmed by his achingly familiar grin but determined not to respond. It would be all too easy to fall for his practised charm, and that was the road to hell, she knew, to her cost. She was a mature adult, she told herself, and had more sense than to make the same mistake twice.

As they drew nearer to their destination Benedict explained the history behind the making of cognac. All along the roadside were the vineyards and invitations to sample the wines that were eventually blended to make cognac. Brandy made anywhere else in the world was not allowed to call itself cognac.

When they finally pulled up in the centre of town, the children who had been half-hearted about the trip were now raring to go. Benedict had fired their imagination, Rebecca realised, something she would not have thought him capable of.

'Why the strange look, Rebecca?' he queried, taking her hand and helping her down from the bus.

'I never had you down as someone who would get along with children,' she reluctantly explained.

Not letting go of her hand, he said, 'I love children; I hope to have my own some day.' A teasing grin spread across his handsome face as he removed his glasses and bent his head down to hers, adding, 'How would you like the job, Rebecca?'

She gasped and pulled her hand from his, a bright tide of red sweeping her delicate features. 'No, thank you,' she muttered, avoiding his eyes, and hastily she began shepherding the boys and girls into some kind of order.

'Embarrassed—a woman of your experience? I wonder why?' His questioning gaze narrowed on her flushed face, and quickly she turned, before he saw more than she wanted him to.

'Kids, follow me,' she instructed, not bothering to answer him.

Rebecca breathed a sigh of relief, as Benedict walked past her, ruthlessly suppressing an unexpected feeling of guilt. She had almost given herself away; she would have to be more careful in future.

The distillery was fascinating, a huge building down by the riverside. They toured the Cognac and Cooperage Museum, which included some pieces dating back to the Middle Ages. Then they boarded a passenger ferry to cross the river to the ageing warehouses, where millions of litres of brandy aged in casks, each row containing the harvest for a single year, going back over a century.

'Goodness, Benedict, the smell in here will be enough to make my lot tipsy!' Rebecca exclaimed as the young guide told them all to sit on chairs at one end of the dark warehouse for a film show.

'Not to worry, sweetheart; as long as I stay sober you'll be fine,' he murmured, sitting down beside her.

When they all finally emerged into the bright afternoon sunlight, Rebecca felt slightly disorientated, but with Benedict's arm flung casually across her shoulder she quickly recovered, and felt dizzy for a completely different reason.

In the visitors' hall the full range of cognacs were on sale, and as Benedict spoke to the guide Rebecca bought a bottle of V.S.O.P. fine champagne cognac. It would be a nice present for Josh and Joanne, she thought, and the least she could do, considering the favour they were doing her.

'Careful. Acquire a taste for the stuff and you lose control,' a deep voice drawled provocatively.

'It's for a friend,' she said quickly.

'A male friend?'

'Yes,' she muttered, wishing Benedict would not tower over her in quite such a domineering fashion.

'Lucky man,' he said curtly, then smiled. 'But perhaps not so lucky. He isn't here and I am.' And, bending down, he brushed her forehead in a brief kiss, before placing his arm possessively around her shoulder and tucking her into his side. 'Have you got all you need? We're holding up the queue.'

Flustered by the sensual warmth of his touch and the unexpected kiss, Rebecca grasped her package tightly with both hands. Was it only she who felt the tension between them? she wondered frantically.

'Yes, thank you,' she said in a tight voice. Her decision of yesterday to play along with the man, as the easiest solution, was beginning to lose its appeal. The effort to hold him at a distance was exhausting and playing havoc with her nerves.

Rebecca stepped into the antique bath full of hot, scented water and slid down until the soft bubbles reached her small chin. Ah, luxury! she sighed. With six females sharing one bathroom she fully appreciated the sacrifice her pupils had made in insisting she could have the bathroom for an hour. But she was not so appreciative of the way she had been forced into dining with Benedict.

For the last two days he seemed to have filled her every waking hour. From their leaving the cognac factory on Tuesday until this evening the time had flown, and she had to admit it had been quite fun.

A reminiscent smile curved her full lips. Today they had driven along the Route Verte to Saint-Fort-sur-Gironde, lunched at the only hotel—Le Lion d'Or—and afterwards they had driven on a few miles to the Moulin de Sap, a large wooded area with a narrow stream meandering through it. In the heart of the wood a timber hut had served as a bar, with a few pedal-boats for hire to explore the waterway.

The children had hired pedalos for an hour and Benedict had insisted she accompany him on one. A chuckle escaped her; she could still see the hurt look of frustration on his face when after half an hour he had tried to turn the boat around in the ten-foot-wide stream.

First they had run aground at the front then at the rear, and in the process one pedal broke. Thompkins and Dodger had come up behind them, hooted at Benedict's struggles then commented cheekily, 'Maybe it's not such a good idea to go on his yacht tomorrow, if his expertise with a pedalo is anything to go by.' Laughing, they turned and left.

When Benedict finally managed to point the boat in the right direction he pushed the one pedal hard, rocking the craft. A jangling sound echoed in the silence as all his loose change fell out of the pockets of his shorts and into the water.

Rebecca had tried for two days to retain some formality between herself and Benedict, but she was fighting a losing battle and at the look of chagrin on his face she had burst out laughing.

His furious eyes met hers, then his lips twitched, he chuckled, and finally his laughter joined hers.

Still smiling, she stepped out of the bath and rubbed her small body dry with a huge beach-towel, then, wrapping it firmly round under her armpits, she headed back to her room.

She sat down at the battered dressing-table and studied her flushed, lightly tanned face in the mirror. She had mixed emotions about the evening ahead. She could not deny the tingling feeling of excited anticipation at the thought of dinner with Benedict. But her common sense told her she was being a fool to risk it.

Later, Rebecca shifted uneasily in the soft leather seat of the white Mercedes, her fingers tugging nervously at the hem of the jade silk dress in a futile attempt to cover her knees. The dress was a mistake. A Bruce Oldfield original, the bodice a wisp of silk that draped in a deep V back and front, fastening at the side with one button, a matching belt circled the waist, the skirt a straight wrapover with two small soft pleats in the front. It had been an impulse buy in the January sales. She must have been mad!

It was the most daringly cut thing she had ever worn, and tonight, when Benedict first caught sight of her, his expression said it all. His face had revealed a variety of emotions, going from the friendly smile he had adopted over the past few days, to shock, then a slight frown, and culminating in what she could only describe as blatant lust.

They had travelled for about ten minutes and Rebecca could feel the tension building in the silence. Her thoughts skidded guiltily between the past and present. They were travelling fast, the road winding between sweet-scented pine forests.

'I don't want to go too far,' she blurted, breaking the silence.

'In that dress? You could have fooled me.' Benedict shot her a sidelong glance, his smile one of wicked amusement.

She flushed. 'I mean I don't want to travel too far. I don't feel right, leaving my colleagues to deal with the children while I gad around,' she explained, ignoring his provocative statement.

'Don't worry, Rebecca. As for going too far, we're almost there.'

The tyres screeched as Benedict swung the car around a corner and into a side-road, and Rebecca was flung across the seat, so she ended up against him. She straightened abruptly, putting some space between them. Her bare arm burned where it had come into contact with his. She told herself it was the ninety-degree temperature of the area, nothing more, but the excuse was wearing thin after two days of frequent such contacts, even to her ears...

'Mechers is a nice little village and the restaurant rather unusual. I think you'll like it, Rebecca, so relax and enjoy, hmm?'

He was right. At first she was puzzled as he drove the car up a hill, through the village, to the top of a cliff overlooking the sea, and parked.

'Where is the restaurant?' she asked dubiously.

'Soon all will be revealed. Trust me.' And, sliding out of the car, he walked round the front and opened the passenger-door, helping her out, with one strong hand cradling her elbow.

The evening air was heavy with the fragrance of flowers mingling with the salty tang of the sea. To her amazement Benedict led her to a small gate, through, and down steps cut into the cliff-face where a large natural shelf formed a wide veranda, with a man-made wall to prevent anyone plunging the hundred and fifty feet down into the sea. The restaurant was a group of caves, carved out of the rock.

'This is fantastic!' she exclaimed. The view of only sea and sky was unreal. 'It's like the secret grotto in a fairy-tale.' She turned shining eyes up to Benedict. 'It's beautiful. Thank you for bringing me here.'

He was not looking at the view, his gaze fixed intently on her lovely face. 'You're beautiful,' he said, his voice husky and vibrant with desire.

For a moment she simply stared at him, aware of a need, a sense of longing, she had not felt in years. He looked overwhelmingly male, dangerously so. Perfectly tailored beige trousers hugged his lean hips, and a complementary short-sleeved silk shirt lay open at his throat, revealing the beginnings of black body hair. 'So are you.' Horrified, she froze to the spot. She had spoken aloud.

Benedict searched her face for a few seconds, and then he smiled slowly. 'We were lovers once, and now I would like to think we're friends. It's not a crime to admit we still find each other attractive.' His eyes slid down to her cleavage where the soft curve of her full breasts was clearly visible, then back to her small face. His golden eyes darkened appreciably. 'I'm giving you fair warning, Rebecca; I want you...'

Rebecca gave a small gasp of alarm and stepped back quickly. She was burning, she could feel the heat through the soles of her sandals to the top of her head. How much longer could she blame the climate?

'Can we eat outside? I like the idea of dining hanging over a cliff...' She was babbling, but his declaration had completely unnerved her.

Benedict's hand grasped her wrist and gently he urged her to sit down at a table overlooking the estuary. 'Yes, we can eat outside.' And, sitting down opposite her, he relinquished her wrist and casually picked up the menu. 'Will you allow me to order for you?' he asked with a faint curve of his hard mouth.

How did he do that? One minute he looked all predatory male, and moments later he was smiling gently. Rebecca moistened her dry lips. 'Yes,' she murmured with a tentative answering smile of her own. Perhaps she had heard him wrong before...

Benedict ordered champagne, and after the first glass Rebecca began to relax; by the second, she was suddenly filled with a sense of adventure. She had been acting responsible and concerned for years, but tonight she felt like a different person, and it was only for the one night. What could go wrong?

Over a delicious meal of asparagus in a creamy sauce followed by a marvellous platter of fresh seafood, the conversation flowed easily. Benedict laughed at some of her stories about teaching and she responded as he regaled her with his account of his first voyage on his yacht.

The sweet arrived, a fantasy of ice-cream and meringue, and as Rebecca licked her lips after the last mouthful Benedict asked lightly, 'Do you still see Mary and Rupert?'

'Rupert took a post at Harvard. I try to keep in touch, but Mary isn't a letter-writer; I've had a card a couple of times——' She broke off, remembering the accuastion she had once hurled at him.

'Yes, I know. I was in America when they arrived; we had lunch. Mary is a very loyal friend—I had a devil of a job persuading her to give me your new address. Why didn't you answer my letter, Rebecca? Had I really hurt you so badly?'

Warning bells rang in her head. 'I'd like a coffee,' she said, attempting to change the subject.

One dark brow arched sardonically, as he met her glance, then he turned to the waiter. 'Coffee for two, and two cognacs,' he instructed, before turning his dark gaze back to Rebecca's wary face. He reached across the table and covered her hand with his... She wanted to snatch her hand back, but thought better of it when she registered his expression.

He was watching her, his intelligent eyes filled with curiosity and a hint of exasperation. 'Why do you shy away whenever I attempt to mention the past, Rebecca? It's almost as though you feel guilty about it. Yet everything that happened between us was all my fault. We need to talk about it. I want to explain. That last day in the study, you were partially right—— '

'Please, Benedict, don't spoil a pleasant evening,' she cut in. 'I can't see the point in raking over dead ashes.' She had enough guilty feelings of her own, and they were

growing larger by the day, the more time she spent with
this man...

'Are they dead?' he demanded tightly.

She swallowed hard and forced herself to ignore the
soft rub of his thumb against her palm, clamping down
on the erotic sensations his lightest touch aroused. He
was much too perceptive; she should have remembered
he was an extremely successful businessman with a razor-
sharp brain, who for a hobby studied the evolution of
the human race. A shiver of apprehension shuddered
down her spine. He would be a formidable adversary to
anyone who crossed him.

'I was very young, when I first met you. Now I am a
very busy teacher who loves her career. I never look back,
but to the future.' She made herself squeeze his hand,
as she smiled deep into his eyes. 'It was great meeting
you here in France; your help has been fantastic. Let's
just forget the past.'

Would he buy it? she wondered, astounded at her
acting ability. Or was it acting...?

Benedict eyed their entwined hands for a few seconds,
then looked up at her with a strange expression.
'Yes...but please just answer one question. Why did
you not answer my letter?'

Letter—he kept going on about some letter, and she
had no idea what he was talking about. 'Perhaps because I never received any letter from you,' she said flatly,
dragging her hands free.

'But you must have done. Mary gave me your address
in Nottingham, and I wrote to you in November, explaining I knew you were innocent of any involvement
in Gordon's death, and apologising.'

'Did you?' she commented, not believing him for a
moment.

'You don't believe me!'

'It doesn't matter.' The coffee and cognac arrived, and she breathed a sigh of relief, but it was short-lived—as she reached for the cup Benedict once again trapped her hand in his. His other hand tilted her chin so she was compelled to face him.

His golden eyes held her captive. 'Rebecca, after we parted I went to France and I did what I should have done in the beginning; I asked my uncle exactly what had happened when Gordon died. He showed me the autopsy report, and he had no doubt at all it was accidental death. He had attended the inquest personally. When I questioned him about my mother's view—that Gordon had committed suicide because his girlfriend had dumped him, and the ''accidental'' verdict had been a kindness to a Catholic family—Gerard quickly disabused me of the notion. Seemingly Mother had been unstable for some time, since the death of her second husband, and my presumed death. When Gordon died she had gone to pieces completely. She had found his diary among his personal effects and jumped at the chance to blame someone for his death. You...'

'Please, Benedict...' Rebecca shook her head.

His hand fell from her chin to the table. 'Please hear me out, Rebecca. When I first met you I had only heard my mother's version of events, and you were right. I did feel guilty. I hadn't been there for her when she lost her husband, and you were correct when you said I wasn't as close to Gordon as I should have been. I did use you as a scapegoat in a way, and I have never forgiven myself for it. I had some crazy notion I could make up for not being there when Gordon needed me. I don't know.'

His hand tightened on hers. 'I met you, and you were so lovely, so full of life...and Gordon was dead.' He shook his head as if to clear his mind, a look of helpless frustration in his dark eyes. 'I want you to know I deeply regret my behaviour. I told you all this in the letter, and

I hoped you could see your way to forgiving me. But you never replied, and I accepted it.'

His eyes told of his deep regret, the sadness in their depths too real for her to doubt him.

'I never, ever got the letter, Benedict,' she said quietly. She believed him, and, looking back, she could see how it might have happened. 'I had a bedsit when I first moved to Nottingham, but after a couple of months I moved into a one-bedroom apartment; perhaps your letter went to the first address, I don't know...' She tailed off as the full import of his confession struck her. If she had heard from him then, would she have done things differently? Would she have told him about Daniel? His explanation had opened up a Pandora's box of might-have-beens, and suddenly she was tormented by doubts.

'Do you believe me now, Rebecca?'

'Yes, yes,' she murmured, but it was all too late, she thought sadly, unable to look at him. The shock of knowing he had tried to get in touch with her and had some excuse for his behaviour was almost more than she could take in, but it did not alter the fact that he had never loved her...

Benedict threw back his head, taking a deep breath of the night air. 'God, Rebecca, I feel as though a huge weight has been lifted from my shoulders.'

She looked up into his handsome, smiling face. The relief on his rugged features was obvious; the trouble was, that same weight had descended on *her* shoulders. How could she tell him he had a son? Did she want to?

She grasped the brandy glass in front of her and raised it to her lips. Slowly she sipped the fiery spirit, trying to compose her shattered nerves. The revelations of the evening took some getting used to. The towering presence of Benedict opposite was a comfort, but also a threat, and she needed time to decide what to do...

Benedict, as if sensing her uncertainty, put himself out to be pleasant.

He told her more about this part of France, as the evening sky darkened and the first stars appeared. There was no one else eating on the terrace, and, with darkness surrounding them and the soft sound of the water lapping against the base of the cliff, Rebecca had the weird feeling that they were the only two people in the world.

Eventually Benedict stood up and drew her to her feet. She shivered slightly in the cool night air, and it seemed perfectly natural for him to put his arm around her and hold her close to the warmth of his masculine body. Still holding her, he paid the bill and led her back to the car. For some reason the journey back seemed shorter, Rebecca thought, as he stopped the car on the road outside the villa.

'It's a beautiful night; shall we stroll along the beach?' he asked quietly.

Maybe it was the drink, but she didn't care and, with a soft smile, she agreed to his request.

Like two children, they dashed across the road hand in hand and down on to the sand. Rebecca kicked off her sandals and Benedict picked them up, carrying them in one hand while his other arm encircled her slender shoulders.

Where the road turned away from the beach the pine woods stretched down to the sand. The scent of pine and the heady feeling of Benedict's hand gently caressing her bare shoulder conspired to break down the protective barriers Rebecca had errected around her emotions over the years. In a dream she wandered along, the sand still warm against her bare feet. Surely she was entitled to one night free of responsibility, one night of magic...?

'Rebecca?' Benedict chuckled softly, and turned her, wrapping her close against him. 'I've been talking for

the last few minutes,' he said into her hair. 'Where were
you?'

'Here.' She smiled guilelessly up into his rugged face
and, lifting her hand, with one finger she gently outlined
his mouth. 'What were you saying?' she murmured.

He caught her hand, and placed it deliberately on his
shoulder. 'I was saying thank you for this second chance,
and promising not to rush you into anything you don't
want; it's enough to know you've forgiven me.' He took
a deep, rasping breath. 'But now I don't know if I can
keep that promise,' he ended huskily.

She wasn't aware she was giving him a second chance
or even wanted to, Rebecca thought muzzily, but, as his
hand drifted down over her full breast, his other hand
tightened convulsively round her waist, hauling her hard
against him. His dark head lowered and his lips found
hers. This was where her play-acting of the past few days
had led her. This was what she had been afraid of, she
thought with a flash of insight, before the warmth of
his kiss deepened and she was incapable of controlling
her own response.

Her arms went around him and he held her tightly
against him. She knew she was playing with fire, but his
masculine arousal was very evident and unbelievably ex-
citing as he moved his hard thighs erotically against her.
Rebecca moaned softly, knowing she should put a stop
to this intimacy, but her senses were swimming with
pleasure, and a restlessness began to uncoil deep within
her.

'God, you feel so good. You don't know what you do
to me, Rebecca. I've wanted you like this for years.'

His rough, deep voice was thick with passion and she
barely registered when he lowered them both to the sand.
She wrapped her slender arms around his neck, her
mouth seeking his; she was floating in a whirlpool of
desire, and she writhed against him as his hand slid inside

the bodice of her dress, his long fingers stroking her hardening breasts. His tongue darted between her lips, exploring her mouth with an urgent passion as his body rocked over hers.

Benedict pulled back and stared down at her; his hands deftly unfastened the belt at her waist and the one button that held the dress in place. 'This damn gown has driven me crazy all night,' he groaned, turning back the silk. 'You're exquisite, Rebecca—tiny, but so voluptuous, absolutely perfect.'

She gazed up at him; the moonlight cast planes and shadows over his dark features but there was no mistaking the burning passion in his golden eyes. She smiled a smile as old as Eve, reached up and unbuttoned his shirt. Then he caught her hands and spread them either side of her lush, near-naked body, her lace briefs her only protection from his hungry gaze.

Slowly he bent his head and with incredible gentleness suckled the hard nub of her creamy breast, first one and then the other, till she thought she would cry out with the ecstasy of it. Allowing one of her hands to go free, he stroked long fingers gently down her flat stomach, easing beneath her briefs to the warm dampness between her thighs.

Her back arched involuntarily. 'Please...' she moaned, her hand gliding down his broad chest to his trim waist, her fingers tugging at his belt.

'Rebecca, my love, tonight I want to love you as I should have done the first time. Slowly, slowly.'

The mention of the first time was like a douche of cold water. Her body clenched in instant rejection, and she grasped his wrist and writhed for a totally different reason, trying to get away.

'Rebecca, no. What is it?' Benedict groaned.

Fighting down the urge to haul him down to her, she cried, 'I'm not protected,' and sprang to her feet.

Fumbling with her dress, she pulled it haphazardly around her. He caught her ankle.

'It's all right, I have something,' he said urgently.

Her breathing was erratic and the ache of frustration was eating at her control. But she saw red at his words. 'Yes, you would!' she cried, and, kicking free, she picked up her sandals and stormed off down the beach, fastening her dress around her trembling body. The swine would be prepared! Shame he hadn't thought of it last time. No, she didn't mean that, she loved her son... But Benedict was rich and powerful, he wanted her now, tonight—she did not doubt that for a minute. But what of tomorrow, and the rest of her life?

No! There was no future for her with Benedict. Perhaps, years ago, they might have made a go of it. But not now. She had responsibilities. It was too late. Wasn't it? She shivered, the night air cold against her hot flesh.

'Rebecca.' Benedict caught her arm. 'Why? We are free, consenting adults!' he exclaimed.

'You might be, but I'm not,' she said sadly.

'The man you bought the cognac for,' he growled.

Suddenly she saw a way out. 'Yes, that's right.'

'I'm sorry, I shouldn't have come on so strong.'

His apology took all the fight out of her. She looked up at him; he was breathing deeply, fighting to control some emotion she could only guess at. 'No, you shouldn't,' she agreed. But he carried on as though she had never spoken.

'I had no right, but I give you fair warning, Rebecca.' And, wrapping her in his arms, he held her still and close to his heart, her head resting on his chest. 'I fully intend to give your boyfriend a run for his money. Your loyalty does you credit, but I want you and I think you want me...'

'I...' She wanted to deny him.

'Shh, Rebecca.' His strong arms enfolded her, soothing, caring. 'Tomorrow we'll spend the day together, and I'm going to visit you in London.'

She sighed. 'Only the children and Mr Humphrey are coming with you on the yacht.' His grip tightened and hastily she explained, 'Miss Smythe and I are spending the day cleaning the villa and packing, ready for an early start on Friday.'

'You work far too hard, little one, but you're right. It's probably better that way. I'll bring the children back so tired, they won't object to staying in the last night, and you'll be free to have dinner with me.'

That was not what she'd meant, but the idea had appeal. This new caring Benedict was someone she could easily grow very fond of. As for visiting her in London, she didn't know... It would present an awful lot of problems. But there was no harm in dreaming for another day. Was there?

'Yes, OK, dinner tomorrow night.'

'Thank you, Rebecca.' Benedict tilted her chin, and kissed her softly swollen lips, before gently tucking her into the curve of his arm, and together, in a peaceful silence, they walked the last few hundred yards back to the villa.

Curled up in her bed, Rebecca told herself she was a mature, sensible woman, and Benedict appeared to be a reasonable man. Perhaps if she told him about Daniel tomorrow night... perhaps they could be friends. She didn't for one minute admit to herself any further interest. She didn't dare...

CHAPTER SIX

SUNDAY evening, school tomorrow, and Rebecca ached all over. With a weary sigh she sank down into the armchair, and closed her eyes. She had been driving solidly for three days, and was absolutely exhausted. Friday across France and back to London. Saturday from London to Corbridge in the north, to collect Daniel, and today back to London.

Thank God it was all over; the past week had been one of the most traumatic in her life, but her secret was still safe. Daniel was fast asleep in the next room, and she could finally relax.

The trouble was, her conscience would not let her. For years she had carried in her mind a picture of Benedict as a totally despicable man, who had wreaked havoc on her young heart for revenge. But in the past week she had seen a different side to him. There was no way he could have faked his obvious delight in the children's company. But most unsettling of all was the letter he had written and she had never received.

She did not question for a moment the truth of his story. She could see all too easily how it had happened. When she had returned to check the mail, Mary had not written until the New Year in response to Rebecca's Christmas card bearing her new address.

Rebecca was forced to question her firmly held conviction that Daniel was better off not knowing his father, and she could not quite dispel the nagging sense of guilt these doubts aroused in her. Wearily she rubbed her

114

aching eyes with her fingers before running her hands through her black curly locks.

What the hell! It was all academic now. She would never see Benedict again. Luckily for her, he had cancelled their Thursday night date; she had been on the brink of revealing all, and making a disastrous mistake. Dolores had told her, when they had returned from the day's sailing, that a Miss Grieves had met the boat and Benedict had gone off with her.

Obviously he had been stuck in Royan for a few days, and by sheer coincidence it had allowed him to apologise for a less than noble part of his life. Having obtained her forgiveness, he was able to carry on with his life with a clear conscience. She ignored the painful stab of regret for what might have been. It was too late. Five years too late . . .

Rebecca looked around her comfortable living-room; the french windows leading to the small garden caught the late evening sunlight. She had bought the ground-floor apartment when Daniel was four months old. The price had been astronomical—not much less than her father's house had sold for—but it had proved worth it. Daniel loved playing in the garden. She had chosen London because, as an unmarried mother, it was easier to get a teaching job in the capital where they were desperate for teachers, and would not enquire so closely into her personal life. Even so, she had stuck a cowardly 'Mrs' in front of her name, though she had never worn a ring.

With the maturity of years she recognised that, at twenty-two, for all her brilliance as a scholar, she had been very unworldly. Her father had always protected her and instilled in her his values. When other girls left home for university, Rebecca had remained with her father, and even after his death she had jumped at the chance of moving in with his colleagues Rupert and

Mary. She had never actually had to stand on her own,
until she was pregnant, so it was hardly surprising that
she balked at actually declaring herself an unmarried
mother. Now she realised it had been a bad mistake. She
had been lucky so far, but eventually Daniel was going
to want some answers about his father, and she knew
she could not lie to her son...

Slowly getting to her feet, she pushed the unsettling
thought aside. It was something she would have to face
in the future, but right now she was exhausted. She re-
trieved the two suitcases from the hall and carried them
straight into the bedroom. The bed, with its pretty rose-
sprigged duvet that matched the curtains and cushions,
looked very inviting. She tightened the sash of her short
towelling robe—she had shared a bath with Daniel—then
resignedly set about unpacking the cases. Gathering a
bundle of dirty washing in her arms, she headed for the
kitchen.

She switched on the kettle, then loaded the washing
machine, added soap and slammed the door shut.
Spooning instant coffee into a mug, she poured the now
boiling water on to it, added a spoonful of sugar—she
needed the energy, she excused herself—and added a
dollop of cream. Re-entering the living-room, she collapsed once again into the armchair and took a long
swallow of the hot, soothing liquid.

A loud knock on the door broke the blessed silence.
Rebecca, draining her coffee, rose to her feet, a wry smile
on her soft lips. Mrs Thompson from the first floor, no
doubt—a widow who adored Daniel and quite happily
looked after him when the occasion arose. Unfortunately,
however, she was a terrible gossip, and Rebecca was not
in the mood tonight.

She opened the door and her mouth fell open in shock.
Conservatively dressed in a dark navy suit, Benedict

stood on the doorstep, his expression grim and somehow menacing.

'Hello, Rebecca, aren't you going to invite me in, old friend?' he drawled mockingly, and before she could speak he had pushed past her and strode into the living-room.

'Wait a minute.' She finally found her voice, and hurried after him. 'What do you mean by barging into my home?'

'Where is he, Rebecca?'

Every vestige of colour drained from Rebecca's face, and she clenched her hands in the pockets of her robe to disguise their trembling. Benedict stood, his powerful presence somehow filling her small room.

'To whom are you referring?' She raised defiant eyes to his face, hoping to bluff it out.

She was prepared for his anger, but the icy fury in his golden-brown eyes froze her to the spot, and his words shocked her by their savagery.

'My son, you bitch,' he ground out between clenched teeth. 'I could strangle you with my bare hands for what you've done.'

In that moment Rebecca could well believe him, and she took an involuntary step back. She had always been afraid this nightmare moment would come some day, but now it had arrived she was struck dumb; not one excuse or explanation came readily to mind.

'Nothing to say, Rebecca, no excuses?' A muscle tensed along his square jaw as he fought to restrain his anger. 'He's mine, Rebecca, isn't he?' he demanded in a deep, savage growl. 'Daniel Blacket-Green, born...'

As he reeled off Daniel's date of birth Rebecca knew beyond doubt that there was no way she could bluff her way out of the situation. How he had found out, she couldn't imagine. 'Who told you?' She heard her voice, shaky with fear, and wondered if it belonged to someone else.

'It sure as hell wasn't you,' he snarled. 'You even labelled him a bastard—no father's name on the register. How could you do that to my child?'

Rebecca dropped her head, flooded with guilt. 'I—I never thought...' She stopped. How could she tell him about the pain, the fury she had felt towards his father when Daniel was born, and her fear that Benedict would claim him, without revealing how much his past treatment of her had hurt? At the time she had walked away from him with her head held high. How could she now expose her true feelings? He would immediately realise just how much she had loved him, something she had vowed never to reveal. She crossed her arms over her waist in a helpless gesture of self-protection. Standing before him like this, the intensity of his anger was like a physical force enveloping her.

'Never thought?' He gripped her shoulders, and gave her a shake that forced her head up to meet his. 'Liar, you thought all right, too damn well.' His eyes burnt black with fury. 'You must have known you were pregnant when I wrote apologising and begging to see you. Didn't you?'

'I never got your letter,' she denied shakily.

He sucked in his breath. 'I've only your word for that.' His fingers bit into her shoulders, and for a second she feared he was going to do her some violence. A long shudder rippled through Rebecca's body, he felt it, and it was as if in some way it helped him regain his control.

A harsh laugh escaped him. 'You're right to be afraid, Rebecca. I treated you badly, but, by God, you got your revenge, denying me four years of my son's life!'

'Daniel is my child,' she finally managed through trembling lips. But it was as though she had never spoken.

'They say revenge is sweet; I trust, for your sake, the past four years were sweet, because you're going to spend the next forty or more paying for them,' Benedict declared with a mocking cynicism that made her blood run cold.

She stared at him in horror. 'What do you mean?'

His eyes held hers unfalteringly. 'I want my son,' he answered softly, 'and—' he deliberately dropped his gaze to where the loose lapels of her robe exposed the soft curve of her breast '—taking you won't be too much of a hardship,' he concluded silkily.

'You're mad. You can't be serious?' she cried.

For a second Benedict's eyes gleamed again with anger. 'Mad? Yes, I was when I discovered I had a son I knew nothing about, but, luckily for you, in the past forty-eight hours I've come to terms with the fact.' He smiled, a brief twist of his hard mouth, totally humourless. 'You and I will be married by special licence in three days, and, to answer your question, I've never been more serious in my life.'

How she would have responded, Rebecca was never to know, because at that moment a small voice interrupted.

'Mummy, can I have a drink of water?'

Benedict's hands fell from her shoulders and he turned towards the boy. If Rebecca had not been in such a panic to get Daniel away from Benedict, she might have noticed the look of vulnerability, the moisture in the man's dark golden eyes.

'Yes, of course, darling.' She dashed across the room to where her son stood in the doorway, dressed in a sleepsuit with a huge picture of Bugs Bunny on the front, and, rubbing the sleep from his eyes with a small fist, he looked utterly adorable—and the image of his father. 'Come to the kitchen with Mummy.' She grabbed his hand, but with the curiosity of the young Daniel refused to move; his sleep-hazed eyes had settled on the strange man.

'Who are you Mr Man?' he asked easily.

Benedict walked over and knelt down beside him. 'I am your daddy, Daniel,' he said softly.

Rebecca gasped in horror. How could he blurt it out like that? Then she choked at the excited expression on Daniel's face.

'You mean, you're my daddy, my very own daddy?'

'Yes, I am your daddy and you are my son,' Benedict assured him solemnly, and gently he reached out and smoothed the black curls from the small sleepy face. 'How about letting me get you that drink of water and tucking you up in bed?'

'Yes, please.' And then, needing his mother's approval and reassurance, he turned large golden-brown eyes up to Rebecca. 'Is he really my daddy? Not like Josh, but a proper daddy, just for me?'

He said it with such longing, tears glazed her eyes. She had not realised how desperately he wanted a father of his own. At two years old, staying with their friends for the summer holiday, he had asked about his daddy and Josh had laughingly told him he would be his daddy—Daniel could share him with his daughter Amy. Oddly enough Daniel had never mentioned it again, and Rebecca had been too much of a coward to bring the subject up.

'Answer him, Rebecca,' Benedict demanded bluntly, rising to his feet to face her, but still holding Daniel's hand firmly.

Her eyes fell beneath the blazing contempt in his. 'Yes, this man is your daddy,' she said softly.

Daniel threw his short arms around the only part of Benedict he could reach—his muscular thigh—and, turning a blissfully happy face up, he said, 'I'll show you where the kitchen is, Daddy.'

Rebecca felt a swift stab of pain like a knife-thrust in her stomach, as two pairs of identical golden-brown eyes smiled at each other. Jealousy at their instant rapport turned her stomach. Daniel had been hers alone, since he was born. Now Benedict had appeared and it hurt to see how instantly Daniel accepted him.

'Daddy, Daddy, I've got a daddy,' his little high-pitched voice sang ecstatically as he skipped across the room, tugging Benedict along with him by a fistful of trouser leg, to the kitchen.

Rebecca collapsed into the nearest chair, and buried her head in her hands. Benedict had appeared and turned her cosy little world upside-down. She couldn't believe it, didn't want to... But the sound of laughter coming from the kitchen was all too real.

Slowly she raised her head, and, taking deep, even breaths, she forced herself out of the panic-stricken shock that had engulfed her for the past half-hour. She was over-reacting, she told herself determinedly. She was a strong, mature woman, who had suffered a good few knocks in her twenty-seven years, and always bounced back. From Gordon, her father's death, to the affair with Benedict, and finding herself a one-parent family.

So what if Benedict did want Daniel? There was no way he could take him away from her; she was his mother... She was worrying unnecessarily. Of course Benedict had a right to be furious on discovering he had a son he knew nothing about. But surely once he had calmed down he would see reason, Rebecca consoled herself. Only a couple of days ago he had stood her up for Miss Grieves; no doubt that same Fiona Grieves who had chased Benedict at Oxford had caught him. His ranting about marriage must be just so much guff. No. She had nothing to fear. She would give Benedict access rights to Daniel maybe once a month, and an occasional holiday...

Her confidence slightly restored, she looked up as
Benedict strolled back into the room, carrying Daniel
on his shoulders. 'It's time you were in bed, young man,'
she said lightly.

'It's all right, Mummy, Daddy's taking me, and he's
going to stay here, and I'll see him in the morning.'

'You...' The 'can't' froze in her throat at the stormy
warning in Benedict's dark eyes.

'I'll talk to you later, Rebecca; now show me the way
to the bedroom.'

Rebecca stood at one side of Daniel's bed, while
Benedict sat on it, reading him a story. That had always
been her job, she thought resentfully. Benedict looked
up at her; the cold mockery in his eyes told her he knew
exactly how she was feeling, and she could not control
the shameful tide of red that washed over her face.

'He's asleep; come along. You and I have some ar-
rangements to make.'

She flinched as his large hand on the small of her back
guided her out of the room. If he noticed he made no
comment, but Rebecca could feel the warmth of his hand
like a burning brand through the soft cotton of her robe.
Suddenly she was intensely aware of her state of un-
dress. She turned quickly. 'If you'll excuse me, I'll get
dressed.'

'Don't bother, you look perfect the way you are.'

She glanced up at him. He loomed over her, huge and
darkly threatening, and suddenly she felt small and very
vulnerable. Cautiously she stepped back, turned and
walked into the living-room.

She dropped tiredly on to the sofa, but kept a wary
eye on Benedict. He removed his jacket, flung it on the
armchair, unfastened his tie and sat down beside her,
his trousers tautening along his muscular thighs as he
stretched his long legs out in front of him with negligent
ease.

'Make yourself comfortable, why don't you?' she prompted sarcastically, unwillingly aware of his hard masculine body only inches away from her.

'Thank you, I will.' And before her astonished eyes he removed his tie, flinging it to join the jacket on the chair opposite, then casually unbuttoned his white silk shirt almost to his waist.

'What do you think you're doing?' she snapped.

His narrowed eyes met hers. 'Exactly what I want to do. And from this moment on that is precisely how our relationship is going to continue. I do as I want! You do as you're told! Do I make myself clear?' he demanded icily, his tone of voice totally at odds with his casual appearance.

She bit back the angry retort that sprang to her lips. Arguing with him would not help the situation; she needed to keep a cool head, it was her son she was fighting for. Slowly counting to ten under her breath, she managed to put her thoughts into some kind of order. Carefully folding her hands in her lap, she began, 'Benedict, I realise we have to talk—obviously it has been a shock for you meeting Daniel for the first time, and I can understand your desire to keep in touch with him.' She studied her folded hands rather than look at him. 'But we are both mature adults, and I'm sure, with a little compromise on both sides, a suitable arrangement can be reached.'

'What would you call a suitable arrangement for a man who has not seen his son in four years?' he queried silkily.

'I'd be quite happy to let you see him once a month and, say, one holiday a year.' She turned her head slightly, watching to see how he accepted her suggestion. His mouth tightened into a hard line. 'Well, perhaps once a fortnight,' she blundered on.

'Try once a day, and you'll be almost there, Rebecca,'
he prompted, a steely note creeping into his voice. 'I
don't intend to put up with anything but your full ca-
pitulation. We will be married, as I told you before, in
three days' time.'

Rebecca's fragile control of her temper snapped.
'Don't be ridiculous; there's no way I'll marry you, and
you can't make me. Daniel is my son...'

'Our son.' Benedict's hard gaze fixed intently on her
furious face, he gave up all pretence of ease, and, with
a speed that shook her to the core, one strong arm
gathered her to his broad chest, and his other hand
curved round her throat, tilting her face to his.

'You would deny me even now—when the evidence of
your own eyes must tell you Daniel and I should be
together!' His eyes were dark golden chips of fury. 'What
kind of woman are you? God, I could still strangle you
for what you have done, but first—first, I'd kiss you
senseless, and make love to you till you begged for
mercy!'

His hand tightened at her throat and for a second
Rebecca truly feared for her life—she had never seen
such inimical anger. So much for her mature adult
compromise, she thought irrelevantly as his head
swooped down and he found her mouth before she could
avoid him.

She struggled, trembling under the savage ferocity of
the kiss, aware of the barely controlled fury in his large
body. The hot, violent onslaught went on and on,
crushing her lips until they felt numb. When he finally
released her, she croaked angrily through swollen lips,
'You hurt me!''

His hand trailed from her throat, sliding under the
edge of her robe. 'Maybe, but it did me a hell of a lot
of good,' he rasped, the anger glittering in his eyes darkening to a much more dangerous emotion.

She tried to jerk away, quivering from head to toe, but his strong arm was like a ring of steel around her, lifting her so she was lying across his lap. 'Oh, no, Rebecca, I haven't finished with you yet,' he muttered, his free hand sliding to cup her full breast, the pad of his thumb stroking the dusky tip.

She was helpless in his hold; her head fell back and she stared into his flushed, taut face, her violet eyes wide with alarm and a rising sexual awareness. She could not move, hypnotised by the intention in his dark, watchful gaze, and the swift heat flooding through her at his continued sensual caress.

Once more he bent his head but this time his mouth was gentle, probing with a skilful, tempting expertise which ignited a flame deep inside her. She opened her mouth, welcoming his thrusting tongue as she kissed him back. She felt his hands wandering from her arm to her thigh, from breast to breast, and his mouth swallowed her low groan of pleasure.

Her own hands, now at liberty, stroked his naked chest, feeling the satin-covered muscle and hair with tactile delight.

He buried his head in the side of her throat, his mouth burning a trail of fire lower. Somehow she was lying on the couch, her robe wide open and Benedict poised over her; as her small hands moved around the back of his head, she could feel the tension of the muscles in the nape of his neck. She curled her fingers into his dark hair, unconsciously urging his head lower.

His strong hands caressed her almost-naked body lovingly, gently. 'Benedict,' she moaned; she could not deny the craving of her body any more. She wanted him with an urgency, a deep-rooted need she had not felt in years.

'Yes, Rebecca, yes,' he murmured, then he caught one taut nipple gently between his teeth. She cried out as he bit lightly, while his hands stroked down over her flat stomach. He raised his head. 'Our son nestled here,' he said throatily, and his large hand spread across her flat stomach, then slid lower to the soft black curls at the apex of her thighs.

'You want me, Rebecca.' He took her hand and laid it against his hard masculine length. 'Tell me, Rebecca, say it.' His mouth touched her creamy breast again. 'Say it...' he demanded unsteadily.

She was trembling all over, every nerve-end on fire, her heart pounding until she thought it would burst. 'I want you, Benedict,' she groaned. Her fingers touched the zip of his trousers, she needed to have him naked... now... She was beyond reason; his hands and mouth were driving her crazy.

His hand caught hers, and for a moment he lay still over her; a little cry of pain escaped her as he crushed her fingers. She felt his body shiver. Why had he stopped her? Then abruptly he sat up.

She smiled up at him, her love-swollen lips pouting for more, only to find him watching her, his teeth clenched in a cruel smile and his dark eyes glittering with pure masculine triumph. Slowly his gaze slid insolently over her naked body,

'You want me, but not tonight, sweetheart,' he drawled. 'You have to marry me first...'

She stared up at him. The light beading of sweat on his brow was real, he was as affected as she. So why? At first her brain, her body, could not accept what had happened, then she realised he was waiting, his intent gaze probing her wide violet eyes, anticipating her re-action. She went hot then cold. What had she done? One touch and she had caved in completely, and Benedict was openly gloating at the fact while brutally rejecting her. Scarlet with humiliation and frustration, she fumbled to pull her robe around her trembling body, shamefully aware of the triumph in his watchful eyes.

'Try and control yourself for three more days,' he taunted.

Rebecca moved her shapely legs to the floor and sat up, with her head bent. She busied herself tying the belt of her robe firmly around her tiny waist. She could not face him; the frustration, the pain was eating her inside, and she wouldn't give him the satisfaction of seeing her distress. Breathing carefully, she forced her screaming body under control.

'No, I will not marry you,' she said quietly, and bravely she turned, making her eyes stay steady on his arrogant face. He hated her; she had seen it in his face, felt it in his anger. She would have to be crazy to even consider the idea.

'You're a fool Rebecca. Does your boyfriend realise how easily you turn on for another man, I wonder?' he drawled cynically, adding 'And to think on Wednesday evening I apologised for rushing you. But now I have proved to my own satisfaction that you're more than ready. You want me... I'm quite prepared to take you along with Daniel. But if you insist, I'll just take Daniel.'

So that was why he had rejected her—to humiliate her, to prove a point... and perhaps to get revenge for her own rejection of him, she thought bitterly. Vengeance was his style, as she knew better than most.

'I won't allow it,' she asserted, and she was not just talking about Daniel; on an unconscius level she was telling herself she would never again allow this man to sexually manipulate her.

'I would have preferred not to go to the courts, but...' He shrugged his broad shoulders. 'I have the power, the money, if that's what you want.'

'No, you can't do that,' she cried, but the implacable look on his handsome face told her he could and would. Worse, she had a terrible feeling he might win. How could she, a single parent who placed her child in a day nursery while she went to work, possibly compete with what Benedict had to offer?

'It's your decision, Rebecca.' He smiled coldly.

The swine knew she had no choice. She dared not risk losing her son; he was her life. And, with that realisation uppermost in her mind, reluctantly she responded in a strained voice, 'All right. I will marry you.' She caught the flash of triumph in his eyes and impotent anger hardened her tone. 'But first I think I'm entitled to know how you found out about Daniel.'

'Quite by accident. The first day in Royan I heard a girl shouting *Mrs* Blacket-Green all over the harbour. I recognised you immediately, and realised I must have misheard. I thought no more about it until Thursday on the yacht, when Dolores, probably imagining she was helping the course of true romance, told me what a wonderful person *Mrs* Blacket-Green was. My suspicion was aroused. Yours isn't a common name, and the likelihood of your marrying a man with the same name must be about a billion to one.'

'Dolores, the mouth,' Rebecca groaned. She should have guessed. Why, oh, why had she ever allowed the children to go on the yacht without her?

'Yes, she's a very talkative young girl. With a little careful prompting I discovered you were either a widow or divorced and you had a young child.

'It struck me as odd. You and I had spent the best part of four days together and yet you never once mentioned you had a child. Thursday evening I called an agency in London and had you investigated. You can imagine my amazement when late Friday I was given the full details of your deceit. I came straight to London, and waited all weekend for you to arrive.'

She stared at the grim lines of his face. For a second she thought she saw pain in the depths of his dark eyes,

ut a moment later she almost laughed out loud at her
oolishness.

His eyes narrowed icily on her small, composed face,
and she shivered at the contempt she read in them.

'Make no mistake, Rebecca, you will never deceive
me again. On Wednesday you become my wife. You have
until then to arrange your affairs.' He stood buttoning
his shirt, picked up his jacket and tie and, turning back
to where she sat frozen on the sofa, he added, 'I use the
word "affair" advisedly. The man Josh—get rid of
him... No one is going to act as a father to my son.'

'But Josh——'

He cut in before she could explain. 'I don't want the
sordid details, just get rid of him—and any other men
you are involved with... Understood?'

What did he think she was—some sex-mad lunatic?
An imp of conscience whispered inside her head that he
had some justification, the way she had reacted in his
arms moments earlier. She stomped on her wayward
thoughts. His opinion was not important; let him think
what he liked—she didn't owe him any explanation. He
was forcing her to marry him, demanding his son. He
had it all... Unconsciously her eyes followed his movements as he slipped on his jacket and fastened his tie.
He was powerful, dynamic, all male, and as her eyes
reached his face she realised he was furious.

'Answer me, damn you!'

She had to search her memory for what he had said.
'Yes, I understand completely.' She rose, her dark head
held high, and moved towards the door. She opened it
and stood to one side. 'I would like you to leave now.'
Her emotions, her life were in turmoil and she could
stand no more.

For a moment Benedict stood, his face flushed with
barely contained rage that she could find no reason for.

Then, like a shutter falling, his dark eyes narrowed expressionlessly on her pale face.

'Perhaps I should call home—a change of clothes would be useful,' he said smoothly. 'Give me your key and I'll let myself in.'

'In where?' she muttered.

'I promised Daniel I would be here in the morning. I intend to keep my promise, but don't worry—I'll sleep on the sofa.'

'But...'

'The key.' Benedict smiled coldly. 'You look haggard. Have an early night and tomorrow we'll spend the day together.'

Like a robot, she crossed the room, picked her bag off the table, withdrew the spare key she always carried, and without speaking held it out. She did not feel she could bear to speak another word to the man, or she would break down completely.

He gave her a long, hard stare, then, swinging on his heel, he left. She heard him move down the hall, the front door open and close surprisingly quietly.

Rebecca heard the thump of her heart in the silence, her legs began to tremble, and she stumbled to the chair and sank down on it, shaking in every limb. Shock, delayed reaction, she thought vaguely. Then the pain that had been lurking on the fringe of her consciousness for hours hit her.

Forcing herself to her feet, she walked stiffly to the dresser and the bottle of whisky left over from Christmas. She had never liked the stuff but now she filled a glass and downed it in a few gulps, the instant warmth that flooded her frozen body bringing some relief, but the chaos in her head could not be stilled. She refilled the glass...

Benedict had stormed back into her life and completely rearranged it. Her own inherent honesty forced

her to admit he had some right. She had always suffered
from a nagging sense of guilt over her decision to de-
prive him of his child. Deep down she had realised that
Benedict would have insisted on marriage if she had told
him she was pregnant, but she had been so hurt at the
time and, yes, passionately angry; her pride would not
have allowed her to marry a man she knew cared nothing
for her.

Now, she had no choice. If she wanted to keep her
son she had to marry his father. It was that simple. Pride
was no longer a factor, and what hurt most of all—made
her thinking mind scream, no!—was the way he had deliberately set out to show her her own weakness. With
cold calculation he had aroused her sexually, then
callously rejected her.

She shivered. She had known from their first en-
counter all those years ago that Benedict had a vast
capacity for revenge, so his behaviour tonight was not
surprising—he was running true to form. Yet only hours
ago, on the evidence of a few days in France, she had
seriously considered she might have misjudged him!

A mirthless laugh echoed in the silence of the room.
A few kind words and a smile, and she was as big a fool
as ever. No, that wasn't quite true, she told herself; he
might be able to make her respond sexually, but never
again would she mistake lust for love... Mechanically
she walked into the kitchen, removed the washing, and
flung it into the drier; the normal mundane chores were
still necessary, even if she was falling apart inside. From
the hall cupboard she withdrew a couple of blankets and
sheets, throwing them on the sofa in the living-room.
The swine could make up his own bed.

Finally she made her way to bed. She would marry
Benedict for Daniel's sake. She would play the part of
his wife to the full, but with the certain knowledge that
she could never love him. She had too much self-respect

to fall in love with a man who had such a vengeful side to his nature. She would never allow him to hurt her again, she told herself.

She ignored the tiny voice of conscience whispering that only a few days ago she had believed his explanation and apology for his behaviour in the past, and forgiven him. She slipped off her robe and crawled into bed, not expecting to sleep, but the exhaustion and emotional turmoil of the last week took their toll, and she slept. Some time later she half opened her eyes at an unfamiliar noise. It's only Benedict, she thought drowsily, and sunk back into sleep, unaware that her subconscious mind had found comfort in his presence.

CHAPTER SEVEN

'MUMMY!' A small body catapulted itself on to her stomach. Rebecca groaned, half awake. 'It wasn't a dream, Mummy, my daddy is here and he helped me dress.' She closed her eyes. God, what had she done?

'Are you awake, Mummy?' A finger poked at her eye.

'Yes, darling,' she muttered, and, turning her head, glanced at the travelling-clock on the bedside table. Seven-thirty. Oh, hell, she'd overslept!

'Coffee and toast OK?' a deep voice drawled smoothly.

'Daddy's made breakfast,' Daniel said proudly, scrambling off the bed, and dashing to his father.

Stunned, Rebecca stared at Benedict. He had obviously showered and shaved—his dark hair was damp and brushed severely back from his broad forehead. Dressed in tan pleated trousers and a crisp cotton shirt, he was all clean-cut, virile male. She squashed her wayward thoughts and tensed as he stood towering over her, a bland smile on his handsome face and a loaded tray in his hands.

'Put that down, and leave—I have to dress,' she said curtly, carefully pulling the sheet up under her chin. Naked beneath the covers, she felt at a hopeless disadvantge.

'Good morning to you too, Rebecca; I never knew you were a grump in the morning,' he drawled mockingly, but did as she suggested, and, with Daniel's hand in his, he added, 'Come on, son, Mummy wants to be alone—women can be funny that way,' and left the room. She felt like throwing something at him, the joint laughter of the two males in her life infuriating her. But worse was to follow.

After hastily washing and dressing in a slim grey skirt and prim white blouse, her uniform for work, she drank the near-cold coffee, ate the toast, and, straightening her shoulders, walked into the living-room. They were sitting on the sofa, talking, but when she moved forward two pairs of identical golden-brown eyes turned on her.

She swallowed on the sudden lump in her throat, and said stiffly, 'Thank you for your help, Benedict, but we must hurry. I have to drop Daniel at his nursery for eight-thirty and get to school.'

The ensuing argument was not pleasant. Benedict insisted they were going to spend the day together.

'I have to work, I can't just walk out on my teaching commitment and, anyway, I like my job.'

'When we're married you won't need to work,' he declared flatly. 'What difference will a couple of days make?'

'A couple of days? I have to give a term's notice!' she cried in exasperation. The time was ticking by, she was going to be late in any case, but suddenly, to her surprise, he capitulated.

'OK, I'll drive you to school, but Daniel stays with me.' And, turning to the little boy, he added, 'How about it, son? You can tell me what you want to take to your new home and help me get everything ready for the removal firm.'

'Are we going to live with you, Daddy? All the time?' Daniel exclaimed with delight.

'Of course; now I've found you I'll never let you go,' Benedict declared in a voice deep with emotion.

Rebecca looked on in impotent fury; the man was leaving her no escape.

'Mummy too?' Daniel queried, rushing to catch Rebecca's hand, suddenly not quite so sure of the massive changes taking place in his young life.

'Certainly, Mummy as well.' Benedict smiled as he moved to place an arm around Rebecca's shoulder, and she froze as he lowered his dark head and quite deliberately kissed her full on the lips. 'Your mummy and I are to be married, we're going to be one happy family.' His golden eyes burnt down into hers, daring her to deny him. 'Aren't we, Rebecca?'

She looked down at Daniel, and the excited anticipation in his little face squeezed her heart. 'Yes, Daniel, it's true.'

At lunchtime, standing in the headmaster's study, with Benedict and Daniel by his side, she had to clench her teeth to prevent herself screaming at the manipulating swine.

The headmaster congratulated her on her forthcoming marriage, and happily waived her notice. The fact that Benedict had presented the school with a new minibus and a large donation to the school fund was obviously worth a lot more than her services.

'You have cost me my job. How dare you do that?' she demanded of Benedict as she angrily slid into the passenger-seat of a gleaming metallic-blue Jaguar. His money could buy him anything, including her...

'It was for your own good. Daniel has spent almost his whole life in nursery school. He deserves some time with his mother,' he said bitingly.

He used the one argument she could not honestly disagree with, and she was immediately on the defensive. 'I spend as much time with him as I can, but I have to earn a living, and I enjoy teaching.'

Benedict shot her a sidelong glance, as he manoeuvred the car through the busy London traffic. 'I'm not suggesting for a moment you've neglected him,' he said quietly. 'In fact you're to be complimented—he's a wonderful little boy and obviously well brought up. But there's no longer any need for you to work. Later, when Daniel is older, I don't mind if you want to work. You're an intelligent woman, I can understand your desire to continue with your career—I'm not a complete chauvinist.'

His attitude surprised her, and the unexpected compliment brought an unwanted flush of warmth to her pale cheeks.

'Daddy is taking us out for lunch, Mummy, to a proper restaurant, and then I'm going to get a toy,' Daniel's voice piped up from the back seat. 'A be-bea...a late birthday present.'

Rebecca looked over her shoulder, thankful for the interruption. Warming towards Benedict was the last thing she needed! 'Whose idea was that?'

'It's all right, Mummy, you're going to get all new clothes as well. Daddy said, when he looked in your bedroom, you haven't enough to fill a suitcase.'

'Exactly what have you been doing this morning?' she demanded acidly, slanting Benedict a frowning glance. Seconds ago she had worried about softening towards him. She must have rocks in her head...

'Relax, Rebecca. As my wife you have a position to uphold, and I couldn't help noticing, when I checked your apartment, you have very little in the way of personal possessions.'

'How dare you?' she spat, absolutely furious at the thought of him mooching through her things.

'Are you fighting with Daddy?'

Rebecca bit her lip in frustration. 'No, darling, we're only talking.'

After that she remained silent, as the full enormity of what she was doing sank into her emotionally exhausted mind.

Meekly she allowed Benedict to lead her into Harrods. In the restaurant she forced the unwanted food down her throat, and tried to smile. She hadn't the heart to spoil Daniel's day. He was so happy. He clung to Benedict's every word. Finally, when the meal was over, she got reluctantly to her feet. Daniel was champing at the bit to reach the toy department.

'Benedict, what a surprise—shopping with the family! How droll.' Fiona Grieves entered the restaurant, loaded down with parcels, just as they were about to leave.

'Something like that,' Benedict responded with a smile for the elegant woman. 'What about you? Is this what we pay you for—shopping?' he teased easily.

'Well, I just had to get something for the wedding,' she simpered.

Fiona was coming to the wedding. Rebecca clenched her teeth to prevent a caustic comment escaping.

'You remember Fiona, Rebecca?' Benedict prompted, an arrogant, mocking smile curving his hard mouth, and she felt like slapping him.

'Of course, but I didn't realise she worked for you, dear,' she responded with saccharine sweetness, her eyes going from one to the other. They made a perfect pair, she thought cynically. The elegant redhead, and Benedict, with a casual suede blouson jacket draped across his broad shoulders, tall and dark, the sophisticated wordly male.

'Didn't I tell you Fiona is an invaluable member of our management team? Has been for some years.'

Why did Rebecca get the feeling that he rejoiced in imparting that snippet of news? Suddenly she felt tiny, completely insignificant in her prim grey suit, and hopelessly out of her depth. She looked around for Daniel;

it was because of him she was putting up with this, she
thought sadly. But where was he? 'Daniel!' she exclaimed worriedly.

Benedict, immediately concerned, said, 'Wait here, he
can't have gone far,' and walked off.

'Well, Rebecca, I suppose I should congratulate you.
You've finally landed him, but I wouldn't get too used
to being Mrs Maxwell. Benedict wants his son. Once the
boy is old enough to do without his mother, you'll be
yesterday's news.'

Sadly Rebecca recognised that Fiona wasn't even being
spiteful—her blue eyes were smiling.

'Make the most of it while you can, and aim for a big
pay-off. I'd do the same in your shoes,' the woman
added.

Before she could comment, Benedict returned with
Daniel in tow. Rebecca bent down and hugged Daniel,
and only when a strong hand gently squeezed her
shoulder did she straighten, raising large violet eyes to
Benedict, a lingering trace of worry in their depths.

'Don't worry, sweetheart, he's safe, and I'm just beginning to realise how hard it must have been for you,
looking after him on your own.' A soft smile curved his
hard mouth, and his golden gaze, wry and strangely
tender, held hers. For an instant an invisible bond seemed
to hold them captive. Then Fiona shattered the moment
as she loudly proclaimed her congratulations once again
and left.

As far as Rebecca was concerned the day went from
bad to worse. In the toy department Benedict got his
eye on a toy car, a perfect replica of a Jaguar that actually had a battery-powered engine. Within seconds
Daniel was in the driving-seat and the assistant was ex-
tolling the virtues of the car. Rebecca was horrifed to
hear Benedict say they would take it. It cost not a few
hundred but thousands of pounds.

'You can't possibly buy that,' she remonstrated with him as he stood at the cash desk. Daniel was still sitting happily in the car, and the assistant had moved out of earshot to deal with the credit card. 'It's obscene, spending so much money. In any case it's more your idea than Daniel's. You're stupid about cars. A Mercedes in France, a Jaguar here... What are you trying to do, start a collection? I will not have my son spoilt; he appreciates the value of money even if you don't.'

'Our son, Rebecca,' he corrected icily. 'For four years you deprived me of all knowledge of the boy. One expensive present is nothing compared to all the birthdays I've missed.'

The return of a beaming assistant silenced her for the moment, but as they left the department she could not contain her anger. 'It's a ridiculous present. Have you thought for one minute where he's going to use it? I presume you do still have the same house in London? Somehow I can't quite see Daniel riding around a marble-floored hall.'

'Next week we're going to look for a place in the country, so you have nothing to worry about...'

Just like that! She was going to live in the country. 'I've already put Daniel's name down for the local infants' school near my apartment.'

'So cancel it. You would like to live in the country, Daniel?' He addressed the question to a grinning little boy. 'Have a dog and maybe a pony?'

'I'd love it, Daddy, and I could drive my car!'

'Bribery and corruption,' Rebecca muttered softly, but the look of joy on Daniel's face silenced her.

In the designer-gown department Rebecca gave up... Benedict brought all his considerable charm to bear on a simpering assistant and Rebecca found herself parading back and forth in front of him and Daniel. Whenever she tried to argue, Benedict was not above using blackmail—a pointed aside to Daniel on the lines of, 'You like Mummy in that, Daniel?' Or, 'That colour is one of my favourites, what do you think?' And naturally Daniel agreed with his Daddy—the man could do no wrong in his eyes. Rebecca was amazed at the camaraderie that had developed so quickly between father and son, and not a little miffed...

The final straw was when they both laughed hilariously at an over-long skirt she tried on. Then Daniel turned to his father and asked, with a worried frown on his young face, 'Do you think I will grow as big as you, Daddy?'

He might as well have added, Or end up a shrimp like his mum, Rebecca thought miserably. She listened to Benedict reassure the young boy, her hard won self-confidence draining away drop by drop.

Later they returned to her apartment, but only long enough to collect Daniel's few treasured possessions; a teddy and a small assortment of toys, plus his favourite duvet with Superman on it. A couple of suitcases easily held Rebecca's few belongings.

Benedict had flatly refused to allow them to spend another night in the apartment, curtly telling her he had no intention of sleeping on a sofa, nor did he intend letting her out of his sight before the wedding.

Her goodbye to Mrs Thompson, her neighbour, was not as painful as it might have been, as Benedict once again turned on the charm, and by the time she left the building Mrs Thompson was convinced that Rebecca was the luckiest woman alive.

Rebecca walked down the aisle of St Mary's church on the arm of Mr James, the butler, a small, ethereal young woman in an exquisite cream silk gown. The bodice, richly embroidered with pearls, was boned and followed the contours of her breast, the waistline dipped, ending

in a flattering V over her flat stomach; the skirt, gently
flared, fell to her knees. A stole of richly embroidered
silk skimmed her shoulders, creating an air of modesty.
Satin high-heeled shoes the same colour encased her tiny
feet, and a small cluster of fresh rose-buds entwined in
her black curls complemented the small posy she carried
in trembling hands.

It was supposed to be unlucky for the bridegroom to
see the bride's outfit, wasn't it? A grim smile twisted
her lips. Benedict had chosen hers—that was some omen
for the years ahead, she thought bleakly.

Hazily she was aware of the guests seated either side
of the long aisle. By some miracle Benedict had arranged, in a few days, a church service, attended by his
uncle Gerard Montaine and his wife, their daughter, her
husband, a niece and two nephews. Gerard's son Jean-
Paul was acting as best man, and there were a few
friends, including Fiona Grieves.

Rebecca had not wanted to invite anyone, but
Benedict, with typical ruthlessness, had overruled her.
So Dolores, her bridesmaid, in a complementary blue
dress, was waiting at the altar, with Daniel, in a velvet
suit, white shirt and bow-tie, by her side.

She caught sight of Mrs Thompson and her lips
twitched in the semblance of a smile. The old woman
was in the front row, wearing the most enormous hat.

Rebecca stood at Benedict's side, barely listening to
the priest, until he reached the part of the service where
she had to respond. She couldn't do it! It was sacrilege.
She turned her head and for the first time since entering
the church she looked at Benedict. She opened her mouth
to say no, but before she could speak his hand gripped
her wrist. His leonine eyes burned down into hers, and
somehow the moment of panic was gone.

Her small hand trembled as he slipped the plain gold
band on her finger, and when she realised she had to

return the gesture and slip an identical band on his finger
her whole body trembled.

Later, at the reception in a smart French restaurant
in Mayfair, Rebecca was still trying to understand what
had happened. Maybe he had the power to hypnotise
people, she thought wryly. God knew, he was powerful
enough in every other way!

She had eaten none of the exquisitely prepared food,
and now the noise and laughter going on around her was
making her head ache. Benedict's constant attention was
adding to her confusion. He was all smiles and gentle
touches, and not one sarcastic remark had escaped him.
She glanced up as he rose to his feet to speak. His speech
was short and witty and very flattering to her. She studied
his strong face for any sign of hypocrisy, but could find
none. What was he up to?

For the past three days the atmosphere between them
had been one of chilly politeness, only Daniel's presence
preventing any outward show of hostility. On Monday
evening, when they had arrived at his house, Daniel could
not contain his excitement and had run around exploring like a whirlwind. By the time Rebecca had finally
calmed him down enough to sleep in his new bedroom,
but with his own duvet, she had been utterly drained.
She had joined Benedict for dinner, and he had sat in a
brooding silence for the duration of the meal. She had
said a curt goodnight and gratefully retired to one of
the guest-rooms.

Yesterday they had all gone to the Tower of London—
Daniel's choice—and she had had to watch the growing
rapport between father and son with mingled feelings of
jealousy and resentment. Last night had been an ordeal
as Benedict's family had descended on the house for an
impromptu party.

'Had enough, darling? Your smile is slipping,' a deep voice drawled as a long arm circled her waist and drew her to her feet.

Her stomach kontted at his touch, and she parted her lips in a patently false grin, gazing simperingly up at him beneath thick eyelashes. 'Sorry, darling.'

Ignoring her sarcasm, Benedict said, 'Have I told you how unbelievably beautiful you look in that dress?' His dark head bent. 'But, even better, very soon the perfect little body inside it will be mine.'

His breath, warm against her skin, disturbed the soft tendrils of hair around her small ear, and she tensed in his hold; his hard, powerful body pressed against her, aroused feelings, a want inside her that her mind had to battle to control. She lowered her eyes, unable to with-stand the stated intent in his darkening gaze. She smiled with relief when his aunt captured his attention and she was free.

'Really, miss, you look absolutely fab... No one would ever guess you were once a teacher.'

For once Rebecca was glad to hear the girlish chatter. 'Thank you, Dolores—I think,' she responded with a grin. 'I'm not sure that is a compliment.' If it weren't for Dolores she would not be in this mess, the thought flitted through her mind, but she could not really blame the young girl. It was obvious Dolores thought this wedding was a fairy-tale come true, and Rebecca hadn't the heart to disillusion her. Politely she moved around the room, hopefully making the right noises, until finally she found herself alone with Gerard Montaine.

'I was hoping to have a word with you, Rebecca,' he said in charmingly accented English.

She looked up at him in some surprise; they had met last night but hadn't really spoken much. 'That sounds ominous,' she teased.

'No, my dear. I wish you both all the happiness in the world, but I do feel I owe you an apology. Benedict has told me all about your previous relationship.'

Her eyes widened in shock, a dull tide of colour running up her face.

'No, please, don't be embarrassed. I just want you to know...'

And to Rebecca's amazement Gerard confirmed everything Benedict had said he had written to her.

'I blame myself for——'

'Really, this isn't necessary,' Rebecca cut in.

'Allow an old man this indulgence. I think it is for me, and perhaps for you.'

She had the oddest feeling that Gerard Montaine understood more about her hasty marriage than most.

'Unfortuantely, on the advice of my sister's doctor, we just ignored her imaginings, hoping they would go away. When Benedict returned, I told him Gordon's death was an accident, and I never realised until later that his mother had told him differently, and he had believed her. It was only after your engagement was broken that Benedict came to me and asked again about Gordon, and told me what had happened. Of course I swiftly put him right, but it was too late—the damage had been done.'

'Thank you,' Rebecca murmured. It was nice of Gerard to bother, but it could not change anything. Benedict hated her for not telling him about Daniel, and he now believed she had got his letter all those years ago and ignored it, simply to get her own back. Not that it mattered what he thought of her, she told herself; Benedict had never loved her... A loveless marriage then, or now, what difference did it make...?

As if her thoughts had reached out to him, he was at her side, his smiling eyes sliding from Rebecca to Gerard. 'Flirting with my bride? Shame on you, Uncle.' And they all laughed; if Rebecca's laugh was a bit strained, nobody seemed to notice.

Then it was time to go. Daniel appeared, pulling on the hem of her skirt, his little face flushed, his bow-tie askew. 'This is the bestest day of my life! Now I have a mummy and a daddy all my own. Josh——'

'All right, son,' Benedict cut in. 'Remember what we arranged this morning; no tears, a kiss for Mummy, and be a good boy for your uncle.'

Rebecca looked from one to the other, and the happy, smiling face of the little boy contrasted sharply with the hard, dark mask Benedict turned on her. She shivered. The easy, laughing bridegroom had reverted to type; obviously the act for his friends was over. She bent and gave Daniel a cuddle and a big kiss, and it was only when he began to squirm impatiently in her hold that she reluctantly released him.

'You left him for a week with your lover—a few days at the seaside with my uncle's family will hardly bother him,' Benedict said in a hard undertone.

Searching his harshly set features, fleetingly a thought crossed Rebecca's mind. Could he possibly be jealous of Josh? Was that the reason for his sudden change in attitude? No. She dismissed the idea. He had just reverted back to his usual sarcastic self.

'Daniel could come with us,' she protested yet again, although she knew it was futile—they had had the same argument countless times yesterday. She could not ignore the suspicion that Fiona had been right. It had already begun; Benedict was trying to wean her son away from her.

His jawline hardened. 'No. For appearances' sake we'll spend a couple of days alone.' He clasped her wrist and for the next few minutes she suffered through the enthusiastic and some ribald farewells.

It was almost a relief to sink into the soft leather upholstery of the hired Rolls, and Rebecca let her head fall
back and closed her eyes. Thank God! The pretence was
over.

But not quite; when the car stopped at the Regent's
Park house Benedict, without a word, picked her out of
the car, swooped her up in his arms and carried her over
the threshold.

'Put me down,' she demanded, but she might as well
have been talking to herself.

'Tradition dictates I carry you,' he jeered, and strode
on up the wide staircase, subduing her struggles as ef-
fortlessly as if she had been a baby. He shouldered open
the door to the master bedroom, and, once inside, kicked
it closed.

Her heart thumped erratically, but Benedict—damn
him!—hadn't lost a breath. Had he always been so huge,
or was it fear that appeared to make him so much larger
and more powerful? 'What are you playing at, Benedict?
There's no one here to witness your act,' she prompted,
the slight quiver in her voice revealing her apprehension.

His eyes bored relentlessly into hers as he slowly
lowered her down the length of his hard body. 'You're
my wife, the mother of my son. As you say, no more
play-acting. Reality starts here and now. I'll wipe the
memory of Josh and all the rest from your mind for all
time, so you know once and for all who you belong to.'

The cold implacability of his words terrified her.
Rebecca felt her feet touch the floor and she tried to
wriggle out of his grasp, but his strong hands curved
over her shoulders.

'Stop it,' he commanded, pulling her so close, she
could smell the lingering traces of champagne on his
breath. 'The dress has served its purpose, but now I think
we can dispense with it.' His fingers pulled the long zip
down the back of her dress.

'Get off!' she cried, grabbing at the front, but she was too late. Benedict's hands slipped the stole off her shoulders, his long fingers curled into the bodice of the dress and pulled it down to her hips, until it fell un-impeded in a pool of silk on the carpet. The speed of his attack dumbfounded her, leaving her almost naked beneath his gaze in the tiniest of lace briefs, a garter belt and stockings.

Folding her arms over her breast in protection, she frantically glanced around the room, searching for some escape. Her eyes stopped at the huge bed and the painful memory hit her like a fist in the stomach; she fought down the feeling of nausea. Nothing had changed in this room in five years, and the memory of the first time they had been here together froze her to the spot. Until that moment she had not really accepted the full con-sequences of the hasty marriage.

Slowly she turned her head. Benedict had removed his jacket, shirt and bow-tie, and one hand was unzipping his trousers, the other caught her shoulder. She raised her eyes to his harsh face, and she knew he had every intention of carrying out his threat.

Without thought she kicked out at him, her small foot connecting with his shin. His sharp intake of breath did not deter her, and, lowering her head, she went for his arm with small pearly teeth, but a hand in her short curls snapped her head back before she could connect.

'Still the same firecracker, Rebecca,' he drawled with mocking cynicism. 'Don't you know better than to waste all that fire on fighting me? You can't hope to win. Much better to save it for bed.'

'I can try,' she cried and, lifting her arm, struck out at his hard face. He caught her wrists and in a flash had spun her around, her back against his broad chest, her arms pinned to her sides.

'I think you need a little soothing, my sweet wife—a touch here.' His hand stroked down her throat slowly to cup her full breast, his fingers kneading softly. 'Now, isn't that better?' his husky voice taunted in her ear.

She tried to kick back at him, but instead he inserted one long leg between hers and she was in an even worse position. 'Let go of me, you brute.' Only by lying back against him could she keep her balance. She closed her eyes, hoping to blot out his presence. She wanted to scream at the unfairness of it. He was so much bigger, so much stronger, and she could feel the first tendrils of desire curling in her stomach. It was all very good telling herself it was only lust and meant nothing, she could handle it, but with her heartbeat racing she was no longer so confident.

'There, there, Rebecca; relax, let yourself go. It's been a long day,' his deep voice mocked her as his long fingers teased a deliberate feather-light path over the soft curves of her breast, circling the tightening peaks, before rolling them sensuously between his thumb and forefinger.

A low moan escaped her as every nerve-end in her body was aroused to a tingling, taut awareness, and still he continued tormenting her. One strong hand slid lower, pressing on her stomach, urging her closer, if that was possible. She felt the hard proof of his arousal at her back and her blood ran hot with wanting.

'Open your eyes, Rebecca. Know yourself, my little wanton,' he whispered, his mouth warm against her throat. 'Look in front of you.' His hand tracked lower, his long fingers stroking inside her tiny briefs.

Her eyes flew open at the intimacy of his caress, and she barely recognised the erotic picture before her. The mirrored door of the wardrobe reflected the two of them locked together. A hectic flush covered her whole body, the large man towering over and around her, broad, tanned shoulders glistening in the late afternoon sun, looked as though he would devour her whole.

'Please, please, stop,' she pleaded, but, even as she pleaded with him to stop, of its own volition her head tilted to allow his lips easier access to her slender throat.

'You want me, Rebecca. You know you do,' he rasped against her velvet-soft skin.

Her eyes flew wide as they met his. The passionate intent in his gaze, the wholly sensual curve of his firmly etched lips, invited her surrender, and to her shame she could not deny him. Need, want, too long denied, ran like molten lava through her veins. Had he always made her feel this way, this aching, all-consuming hunger? she wondered, arching back against him, trying to turn her head.

'Yes, yes—oh, yes,' she moaned as he finally turned her around, and his mouth captured hers in a greedy, insatiable kiss, a currrent of overwhelming emotion melting her bones.

He swung her up in his arms, his lips finding her breast as he carried her to the waiting bed. His weight came down on her, while his hands still explored every curve and plane, every tiny inch of her, dispensing with her remaining few clothes with an erotic expertise, slowly curling the stockings down her shapely legs, with scorching kisses trailing in their wake, and when he treated her garter belt and briefs in the same way, his mouth hot on her moist, intimate flesh, she cried out.

'Please...' She did not know if she was begging for him to continue or stop, her body arched like a bow-string, her slender arms curved around his shoulders, her fingers tracing the muscle and sinew of his broad back.

Benedict pulled away for a moment, shedding his pants, then she felt the glorious naked weight of him in every pore of her body as he lowered himself over her, sliding between her legs.

He took her with a sudden, passionate thrust, and for a second her small body clenched in unexpected discomfort. Benedict stilled inside her for a moment, allowing her body to accept him, the tension to build... Then he moved, his deep, slow strokes filling her completely, and suddenly her fears vanished in a flash-flood of passion. She clung to him, her nails digging into his flesh, shuddering violently in a mind-bending ecstasy she had only glimpsed before.

His powerful thrusts accelerated to a pounding rhythm that she instinctively matched. Finally, when she thought the tension would consume her, her burning, throbbing body clamped to his, convulsed in an erotic dance of life. Benedict jerked against her with a guttural, rasping sound of completion, his large body thrusting violently into the quivering silken softness of hers.

It was a long time before she stirred. Her mind seemed incapable of registering the enormity of what had happened, while her body pulsed languorously beneath the weight of Benedict's.

'Are you all right?' he rasped, and, easing himself up on his elbows, he added, 'I'm too heavy for you.' His eyes searched her flushed face, her swollen lips and lower to her full breasts. 'You're so tiny and so beautiful, my perfect, passionate little Venus.' His smile was one of pure masculine triumph. Rebecca did not see the flash of some other emotion, as she briefly closed her eyes in embarrassment.

'Get off me,' she whispered, consumed with shame at the ease with which he had seduced her. His broad shoulders flexed, and a vivid image of the two of them earlier, reflected in the mirror, flashed in her mind. The calculating way he had made her aware of her own sensuality made her burn with resentment. 'I hate you,' she muttered, turning her head away. Her brain registered the time on the bedside clock. God, it was barely an hour since they'd left the reception! Still daylight. She would never forgive him, never...

Benedict chuckled. 'Ah, Rebecca, you can hate me as much as you like, sweetheart,' he mocked as his lips sought the soft line of her neck, 'as long as this exquisite little body knows its master.' His hand stroked over her breast in a light caress, and to her horror she felt the stirring of renewed arousal.

Hands that had clung to his broad back only minutes earlier pushed at his damp chest. 'You're an animal,' she cried. 'You could have waited.'

'You can call me all the names under the sun but it doesn't alter the fact you wanted me.' He ran a taunting hand down over the naked curve of her waist and thigh. 'And still do.'

'No,' she choked as he quickly caught her failing hands and pinned them either side of her head. She shivered; his powerfully body was poised over her like some avenging angel, but the dark glitter in his golden eyes was pure devil.

'Yes, perhaps you're right, Rebecca, maybe I was a little hasty,' he drawled lazily.

'You were!' she exclaimed. She didn't trust his suddenly agreeing with her.

'Ah-ha...' His dark head lowered and once again his mouth sought hers. She was too weak to fight him, and she squeezed her eyes shut, as he murmured teasingly against her lips, 'This time I'll take you slow and easy, pure pleasure. Hmm?'

It was dark when Rebecca next opened her eyes. For a moment she was disorientated; her limbs felt heavy, her body aching, and when she moved her arm brushed hard, warm flesh. She stiffened, hardly daring to breathe,

as memory returned. The deep, steady sound of
Benedict's breathing told her he was asleep.

Moving cautiously, she eased out of the bed; with only
a pale moonlight to guide her, she silently crossed the
soft carpet to the bathroom. She closed and locked the
door behind her with a shuddering sigh of relief.

A quick look around the extravagantly furnished room
and she blushed at her own naked reflection in the mirror
on the wall. The marks of Benedict's lovemaking were
clear to see on her soft skin. Heat surged through her
as she recalled the long, slow assault on her senses.

The incredible intimacies he had subjected her to
should have horrified her, but to her shame she had responded with a wild abandon, and returned the favour.
She had explored his hard-muscled body with a tactile
delight, glorying in his muffled groans, fascinated by his
big masculine form.

She shook her head to dispel the erotic images and
walked into the shower-stall; turning on the gold-plated
tap, she stood under the cleansing spray. Methodically
she washed every centimetre of her flesh, in a vain attempt to wash away the memory of her husband's
possession . . .

Much as she would have liked to deny it, he had possessed her absolutely and, worse, deep down in the
innermost part of her being she knew she had wanted,
even welcomed his sensual mastery. She tried to excuse
herself. It was because she had been celibate for so long—
any man could probably have aroused her. But she knew
she was lying. It was only Benedict who had the power
to make her fall apart with just a kiss, a caress. She had
no defence against him, and sadly she realised she
probably never would.

Rebecca closed her eyes and allowed the warm water
to work its soothing effect on her tired body. She didn't
hear the shower door open, and almost jumped out of

her skin when a deep, masculine voice asked throatily, 'Mind if I join you?'

'No!' she exclaimed, stepping out of the shower and bang into Benedict. She pushed at his chest, putting some space between them, her pulse picking up speed as she tried to subdue her awareness of his large, hard body so close beside her.

'Pity, it can be fun,' he drawled sensuously.

She glanced up and flushed at the knowing gleam in his eyes. She looked down but the tiny black briefs he wore were barely decent. She gulped and stared straight ahead, but his broad chest, the darkly angling body hair, was no less intimmidating.

'No? Then here—allow me.' And, wrapping a large towel around her naked form, he began towelling her dry, his big hands strangely gentle.

'I can do that myself,' she said in a muffled voice, as he brought her body into close contact with his, holding her small, very wet head to his chest while he briskly rubbed her hair. The intimacy of the situation completely unnerved her.

'Why bother when you have a willing slave?' he drawled huskily, and, dropping the towel to the floor, he folded her in his strong arms, bringing her body into an even more intimate fit with his.

She squeezed her eyes tightly shut, trying to hold back the tears of self-pity. It was so unfair, she thought helplessly. If she was six feet tall, she would punch him in the nose, but fighting him was a futile exercise, as she had learned to her cost. She hated being so defenceless; she was a strong, mature woman, used to living her own life, and in a few short days it had all been taken from her.

Benedict tilted her chin with one finger, his eyes narrowed, dark and intent on her pale face. 'Are you all right?'

She felt his body stir against her and the evidence of his arousal seemed like the ultimate insult. A blind anger consumed her. 'No, I'm damn well not,' she said defiantly, her eyes misted with tears.

'You feel perfect to me.'

She spun away from his restraining arm. 'And you feel like a sex maniac to me,' she snapped back, her violet eyes no longer misty, but furious.

The masculine line of his mouth quirked with amusement. Reaching out a hand, he caught her arm, and, placing his finger over her lips, so that her eyes sparked even more angrily, he said, 'You can blame me for a lot of things, Rebecca, but the sexual chemistry between us is a mutual explosive force. You can't blame me for being a man.' His eyes assumed a mocking gleam. 'And I suggest you stop blaming yourself for being a woman.' His gaze angled down her naked body, taking in the soft, faint bruising of her flawless skin, the deeper pink areolae of her breasts, where not long ago he had suckled, then back to her furiously flushed face.

'Look at yourself. The signs of our mutually satisfying lovemaking are traced in your fair flesh, my little firecracker. So let's not pretend. If I'm a sex maniac, you were with me all the way.' He dropped her arm and, cupping her face in his hands, he pressed a swift, hard kiss to her swollen lips. 'So what does that make you?' he gibed, and with an arrogant smile he released her and, stepping past her, entered the shower cubicle.

The sound of his laughter was the last straw. 'Why, you egotistical bastard!' she exploded, but the sound of running water muffled her words. Spitting nails, Rebecca grabbed another towel and, wrapping it tightly around her chest, she slammed out of the bathroom. The fact that Benedict was right did not help her temper at all.

Returning to the guest-bedroom she had used for the past couple of days, she was even more infuriated to find all her clothes had been removed; she stormed back to the master bedroom, and flung open drawers. It was just as she had suspected. The housekeeper had transferred all her clothes.

Cursing under her breath, she found a bra and matching briefs; from the wardrobe she took the first thing she touched: a blue cotton blouse with a matching blue and cream patterned skirt—one of the outfits Benedict had bought. Hastily she dressed, her stormy eyes lighting on the clock. Ten. And suddenly her stomach growled. She was famished.

'Going somewhere?'

Rebecca stiffened at the blunt question. 'Downstairs to get something to eat,' she flung tersely. She glanced at Benedict. He was wearing only a brief towel, knotted low on his hips. Suddenly the room seemed far too intimate. She wanted to run, and bristled defensively, as he strode towards her.

Noting her reaction, his golden eyes narrowed in a brief frown. 'Relax, Rebecca.' He reached past her and drew a navy silk Paisley robe from the wardrobe. 'I've no intention of starving you.' And, dropping the towel to the floor, totally unconscious of his nudity, he stood in front of her and slipped on the robe.

'How reassuring,' she gibed, trying to ignore the potent appeal of his naked, sun-bronzed body.

'In any way,' he added provocatively, the sensual promise in his eyes unmistakable, and she darted out of the room like a scared rabbit.

The kitchen was immaculate stainless steel, all tiled, and with every known gadget. Rebecca looked around, and longed to be back in her own kitchen. It was never likely to happen—not for some years, if Benedict had his way.

Yesterday, she had reluctantly listed her home with an agent as available to rent. She was lucky, she supposed, Benedict had not insisted she sell it.

With a tired sigh, she crossed to the refrigerator, opened the door and peered inside. A wry smile curved her lips. Mrs James, the butler's wife and Benedict's housekeeper, had been very efficient. On the top shelf was a tray of cold cuts, and salad, plus a bottle of champagne.

She slammed the door on the champagne and meat; instead she took an egg from a basket on the counter and, turning on the gas cooker, she splashed some oil into the frying-pan. So what if fried food was fattening? The way she felt at the moment she couldn't give a damn! She popped two slices of bread in the toaster and had just cracked the egg into the hot fat, and taken a spatula from the rack beside the cooker, when Benedict walked into the room.

'Fried egg? Not a very romantic wedding supper,' he said with a smile. 'Still, if that's all you can cook, I suppose it will have to do.

'I'm not your slave,' she said angrily.

Her flash of temper seemed to amuse him. 'Temper, temper. Did your mother never tell you the way to a man's heart is through his stomach?'

She turned slightly. He was dangerously close, she could see the fine lines spreading from the corners of his eyes, and the amusement in their depths infuriated her. 'You're the only man I know who makes me angry, and, as for finding the way to your heart, if I did I would cut it to pieces,' she snapped.

Dark eyes met hers, deep and unfathomable, successfully masking his thoughts, but the hard line of his jaw clenched imperceptibly. 'I see you've drawn the battle-lines,' he said sardonically.

Mutinously she stared at him. He was wearing the Paisley robe, his legs were bare and the V between the robe's lapels revealed the soft black mat of hair on his chest. The sheer masculine strength of the man hit her like a physical blow.

Her hand holding the spatula trembled, and she was furious at her own weakness. The toast popped and thankfully she turned her attention to the food. She slid the spatula under the fried egg, trying to ignore Benedict's overpowering presence.

'Make mine over easy,' he murmured, his lips brushing her ear.

Whether it was the brush of his lips, his warm breath on her skin, or just the mockery in his tone that made her snap, she didn't know. But quite deliberately, instead of turning the egg over in the pan, she turned around and turned it over his head.

The look on his rugged face she would carry to her dying day. Incredulous did not begin to describe it. His dark brows drew together with puzzlement, as the yolk broke and trickled over his broad forehead, and down his nose.

Rebecca couldn't help it; her lips twitched, he looked so stunned and so funny. She could not resist gibing, 'An original Eggs Benedict!' and the laughter bubbled out, as she watched the hard white bounce off his shoulder and splatter on the floor.

CHAPTER EIGHT

'REBECCA!'

Benedict's roar stopped the laughter in her throat. Suddenly she was confronted by an absolutely furious primitive male animal. Nervously she looked around for a way of escape. She flinched as Benedict's hand reached past her and turned off the cooker; his other hand caught hers, and relieved her of the spatula, throwing it contemptuously over his shoulder. It landed with a clatter on the tiled floor.

'Now Ben—— Ah!' His name changed into a terrified squeal as he caught her shoulders, shoving her back against the refrigerator door.

'Eggs Benedict, you said, you little witch. Well, now you are bloody well going to eat it.' His head bent, his mouth crushing hers as his hard body slammed into her, sending a shock wave of fear mingled with a feverish pleasure jetting through her veins.

His hands were everywhere, moving from her breasts to hips, to thighs, in a savage exploration. He rubbed his face across her breasts, tearing her blouse open in the process. With his teeth he broke open her front-fastening bra. Rebecca swayed on her feet, her knees weakening as he pushed her skirt up around her waist and ripped her silk briefs away from her body.

Helplessly she clung to his wide shoulders, her body throbbing with a mercurial flash of aching desire, as he lifted her bodily off the ground, burying his face between her full breasts, his fingers digging into her rounded bottom as he lifted her higher. When his teeth bit the sensitive tip of her breast, her shapely legs, of their own volition, snaked around his lean waist. He entered her, driving repeatedly into the hot, wet centre of her womanhood. The sheer voracity of their coupling stunned her brain and finally she cried out, her slender body shaking in tumultuous release as Benedict thrust again, his large frame shuddering in a mutual climax.

She came back to reality when her feet touched the floor; she was aware of the icy coldness of the refrigerator door at her back while inside she was burning. Rebecca could not believe what had happened. They had come together in a blazing angry passion that had utterly consumed her mind. If anyone had told her yesterday that making love shoved up against a refrigerator door was erotic, she would have laughed her head off...

But now, raising her flushed face to look up at Benedict, she wasn't laughing. His dark golden eyes, full of remorse and something else she dared not put a name to, roamed over her delicate features. Lust no longer seemed the right word, she thought wonderingly.

'God, Rebecca, I'm sorry...' His deep chest heaved, and she rested her small hand on the dark, damp curls; she could feel the still rapid pounding of his heart beneath her finger tips.

'It's all right...' she breathed shakily.

'It isn't all right, damn it!' Benedict rasped. 'I swear I've never behaved this way with any other woman in my life.' He brushed a none-too-steady hand through the black hair falling over his brow in a gesture of bewilderment. 'You scramble my senses, enrage and infuriate me until I lose all self-control. You're so lovely and so tiny.' His dark eyes grazed over her slight but voluptuous body. With a snort of self-disgust, he began fastening her tattered blouse, his strong hands smoothing her rumpled skirt down over her slender hips. 'God,

what a wedding night! I'm sorry, Rebecca. I behaved...like an animal. I'm afraid...I hurt you.'

She smiled at him tenderly. 'No, no, you didn't hurt
me.' She wanted to smooth the worried frown from his
forehead, cuddle him as she would Daniel when he dis-
played that exact same expression—a mixture of sorrow
and guilt. Her violet eyes widened to their fullest extent.
His lovemaking could never hurt her... She loved him...
She could fool herself no longer. It wasn't lust or duty,
as her rational mind had tried to insist, but love, glorious love... She exulted in the discovery, her glowing
face turned to his, and then his voice pierced her
consciousness.

'Maybe not this time, but the way I feel about you,
one day it's bound to happen.' He spoke slowly, his
words husky and faintly slurred, as if he was speaking
his thoughts out loud without knowing it. 'I should never
have married you.' He brushed the back of his hand
across his eyes in a weary gesture.

Rebecca stared up at him, incapable of tearing her
gaze from his attractive but suddenly haggard features.
Her hand fell from his chest, her fingers curling into
fists at her side. Hysterical laughter bubbled in her throat
as the hopelessness of the situation struck her. She had
finally admitted to herself she loved Benedict, and
probably always had. While he had reached the totally
opposite conclusion; he hated her and should never have
married her.

'Benedict...' she said helplessly.

His face hardened into a familiar, impenetrable mask.
'You'll have to stay here for a while, but you don't need
to worry—I won't force myself on you again. I'll buy a
house in the country for you and Daniel. I'll stay in town,
and with your permission visit occasionally.'

She shivered, briefly closing her eyes against the pain.
He had it all cut and dried.

'You're cold, Rebecca, go to bed.' He turned to gesture around the kitchen. 'I'll clear the mess ... we'll talk tomorrow.' His cold, clipped voice chilled her to the bone.

Slowly she walked out of the room, a wave of icy desolation sweeping through her; on trembling legs she mounted the stairs to the bedroom. Talk! What was there to say? She undressed and washed before she got into bed, but she couldn't sleep.

She was blinded by tears. They had been married for a few short, chaotic, frenzied hours, and in that time her emotions had run the gamut of just about every feeling known to the human race. Was it only three days ago that she had sought the sanctuary of her own bed in her apartment, upset at having to marry Benedict, but consoling herself with the knowledge there was no way she would ever love him? *Ergo*, there was no possibility of him hurting her again ...

In her conceit she had considered herself far too realistic, too intelligent, to ever make the same mistake twice. There was no way she could love a man who had such a ruthless, vengeful side to his nature.

Yet now, lying in the bed on which they had made love only hours earlier, she could not deny she loved him ...

Rebecca jolted awake, as a heavy arm crashed down on her. It felt like a lead weight cross her breasts. She turned her head on the pillow and in the gloom of the dawn light she made out the shape of Benedict beside her. He was lying on his stomach and his long arm was effectively pinning her to the bed.

Groggily she remembered coming to bed last night, tormented by the knowledge that she had fallen in love with her husband. She must have fallen asleep. She hadn't heard him join her.

She tensed, as he grunted something unintelligible. Was he waking up? No, but he was making it very difficult for her to breathe easily. Warily she tried to push his shoulder, and her hand stilled on his flesh. His skin was burning where she touched it; suddenly she was aware of the unnatural heat exuding from his large body. She heard him groan her name and instinctively stroked her hand caressingly over his shoulder. His skin was wet with perspiration...

Suddenly it struck her that this was no ordinary sleep; his breathing was heavy and laboured, interspersed with guttural words she could not decipher. Was he having a nightmare? Somehow she had always considered Benedict as some exalted, superhuman being, but now, as he unconsciously held her captive, she was struck by the realistion that Benedict suffered from the same frailties, was susceptible to the same dark fears, as the rest of the human race.

It was impossible for her to lift his arm, so carefully she wriggled up the bed until she was in a sitting position, then gently, with both hands, she managed to lift his arm from her legs, and slide out of bed. She switched on the bedside light, pulled on her robe and turned to stare down at him, her delicately arched eyebrows drawn together in a worried frown. This was no ordinary nightmare; something was wrong, badly wrong with him.

As she watched he flung himself over on to his back, the bedclothes twisting around low on his thighs. His muscular chest rose and fell erratically, his face was flushed and his dark hair, wet with sweat, was plastered to his brow.

'Oh, Benedict,' she whispered; sitting down on the side of the bed, she reached out and swept his hair back from his forehead. The heat was phenomenal, his temperature must be sky high, she thought fearfully.

She was reminded of Daniel when he had suffered from measles once, and her heart squeezed with love for him. He looked so helpless. Worriedly she chewed her bottom lip. It was all well and good staring at him with cow eyes, but what was she going to do?

She called his name, but his eyes remained firmly closed, his dark, curling lashes glued to his skin with moisture. Was it a summer flu? she wondered. But as the thought occurred he began to shiver, his muscular torso shaking as if in the grip of some virulent fever. Struggling with the tangled sheets, she managed to pull them up to his shoulders, her hand sliding over his sweat-slicked chest, when shockingly he raised his head, his eyes wide open, and his hand caught her wrist in a grip of steel.

'Rebecca, Rebecca, don't leave me, please. I...' His mouth worked but no sound came out.

'It's all right, Benedict, I'm here, but you're ill.' Who was his doctor? She had married him, slept with him, but in reality she knew so little about him. 'You need a doctor.' She saw his throat move as he swallowed hard.

'No, no doctor.' His dark eyes burned with a feverish light. 'Fever—cabinet in bathroom.' The words took all his strength, his eyes closed and his head fell back on the pillow.

She leant forward and gently replaced the covers around his now completely still form, panic clawing at her heart. Fever! What kind of fever? Ovbviously he had suffered from it before, but as far as she was concerned it could be anything. She sat by his side for a few minutes longer. Was he asleep or unconscious? She didn't know, but she couldn't sit here doing nothing.

Jumping to her feet, she shot into the bathroom, opened the large cabinet above the washbasin, and groaned, 'Oh, no.' There were half a dozen different bottles, and with trembling hands she painstakingly read the labels. Four she could dismiss as proprietary brands of pain-killers. But she was still left with two bottles. She breathed a sigh of relief as she noted the doctor's name on both.

Dashing downstairs, the bottles in her hand, she raced into Benedict's study; a desk diary and a personal telephone directory lay on the large oak desk. In a matter of seconds she was dialling the telephone nunmber of a Dr Falkirk.

A gruff, sleepy voice answered her; briefly she explained the position, and was told to check—one of the bottles should contain chloroquine.

She heaved a deep sigh of relief. 'Yes.'

'Good. No need to panic; we've been through this countless times before. Mr Maxwell *will* forget to take his tablets Mrs James.' Rebecca didn't bother to correct him. 'Give him one three hundred milligram tablet with a glass of water immediately. Keep him comfortble, sponge him down, plenty of liquids, and I'll be there directly after morning surgery.'

She wanted to scream at the man to come immediately, but common sense told her it would do no good. Quickly she ran back upstairs, and filled a tumbler of water in the bathroom, before entering the bedroom. She choked back a sob. Benedict was lying as she had left him, and the high colour in his cheeks, the perspiration running down his brow, brought tears to her eyes.

'Oh, Benedict, please,' she murmured in anguish, 'wake up!' With the tablet in one hand and the glass of water placed on the bedside table, she sat down by his head and slid one arm beneath his massive shoulders. How she got the strength to lift his heavy body, she didn't know, but for a moment his eyes opened, and his glazed, feverish glance skidded over her.

'Rebecca . . . you stayed,' he groaned.

'Shh, don't talk. Swallow this.' And, placing the tablet against his lips, she watched as he weakly opened his mouth. Supporting his head, she picked up the beaker of water. 'Drink, Benedict.'

She breathed a sigh of relief as his throat worked, swallowing the liquid in great gulps. His head fell back and down against her breast, a dead weight against her. But he was still awake, his sweat-drenched features contorting as, in a delirium, he rambled remorsefully and then raved angry, disjointed sentences that made very little sense to Rebecca.

'Gordon, I'm sorry... Betrayed you... Should have made sure... Sorry, sorry... Guilty, Rebecca.' He flung himself over on his side, out of her arms, his back towards her. 'Not the only reason...' He was breathing unevenly as he tossed about in feverish agitation. The way he cried her name brought a lump to her throat and confirmed her earlier fear. She was guilty in his eyes. Obviously he was sorry he had ever married her. What else could it be?

She leant over him; he might hate her tomorrow, but right now he needed her... and that was enough for her. Her tender heart ached to comfort him, when suddenly he flung hinmself over on to his back. Surprising her with his strength, he grasped her hands, holding them to his damp chest; she could feel his heart thundering erratically, and she battled to hold back the tears. It hurt her almost physically to see him this way.

His eyes, wide and surprisingly brilliant, bored into hers. 'Gordon... Rebecca. A guilty passion... I had no right. You understand... tell me you understand...'

Rebecca didn't, but she could not bear the lost, pleading look in his glittering eyes. 'I do understand, Benedict, and it's all right; please try to rest.' She blinked back the tears stinging her eyes.

Benedict, in a brief moment of normality, searched her lovely face. 'You're crying... for me, Rebecca?' A pitiful attempt at a smile twitched his full lips. 'You will stay.' And, as suddenly as he had awakened, his grasp on her wrists weakened and he fell back aginst the pillow, she hoped asleep and not unconscious.

Rebecca hurried to the bathroom and returned with a basin of water, sponge and towels. She had no idea how long she sat watching him, occasionally sponging his face, his chest; the bedclothes were damp. She would have to change them. But how? And all the time her troubled mind tried to make sense of his rambling.

What had he meant? 'A guilty passion' and 'not the only reason'. If she could decipher his ravings, she might understand him better. The ringing of the doorbell intruded on her troubled thoughts. The doctor! Carefully she stood up, and smoothed the bedclothes over Benedict's broad chest. He did not stir, he appeared to be deeply asleep. She flew downstairs and opened the front door.

'So Mr Maxwell has been naughty again.' The bluff Scots accent went well with the short, stout man who walked past Rebecca into the hall. He turned. 'You're not Mrs James.' His grey eyes, a hint of disapproval in their depths, searched her pale face.

'I am Mrs Maxwell, Benedict's wife.' It was the first time she had said the words out loud and it gave her a certain pride. 'Mrs James is on holiday,' she went on to explain, holding out her small hand in a conventional greeting.

Dr Falkirk positively beamed, his plump hand shaking hers so heartily, she could feel the vibration to her shoulder. 'Well, so the old devil finally got married. My congratulations. When was the wedding?'

Rebecca could feel the heat rising in her face. 'Yesterday,' she responded quietly. 'But please, don't you

think we should go up to Benedict?' To her astonishment the doctor started to laugh as he headed for the
stairs.

'Well, that could explain this attack—emotional upheaval is a prime cause of activating this particular
tropical disease, and very few things in life are more
traumatic for a man than getting married. Come on,
lass, let's have a look at him, and don't you worry. He'll
be as right as rain in a day or two.' Still chuckling, he
strode into the bedroom.

She stood by the bedside while the doctor took his
patient's pulse, lifted his eyelids and examined his eyes,
all without Benedict moving.

'Yes, just as I thought. He picked this up in Brazil,
you know. There are hundreds, no thousands, of tropical
diseases, a lot the medical profession don't even have a
name for. But we sorted this out the first year he was
back in England; nothing to worry about. Probably in
all the excitement leading to the wedding he has forgotten to take precautionary measures. You've given him
the dose of chloroquine? What time?' he asked briskly.

'Yes.' She looked at her wristwatch—ten-thirty in the
morning—and it was then she realised she was wearing
only a robe. Dear heaven, what must the doctor think
of her? She blushed scarlet, mumbling, 'I don't know.
About ten minutes after talking to you.'

'Hmm, we'll say six-thirty. Let him sleep for now, then
two more doses today, but tomorrow and the following
day he'll only need one; that will do the trick. One tablet
a week is all it takes to prevent this type of occurrence,
but he must have forgotten again.'

He hesitated, his grey eyes sliding over Rebecca from
head to toe, taking in her slight stature, and very red
face. 'If you are at all doubtful about looking after him,
I could bring in a nurse, or arrange for him to be taken
to a private nursing home. It wouldn't be the first time.'

'No. Oh, no!' she cried. 'I can manage, honestly I can.' Benedict needed her, and it was probably the only chance she would ever have to lavish all her love and care on him. No way was she going to allow some stranger to take her place.

'Excellent.' Dr Falkirk smiled. 'But if you're at all worried call me in the morning. Try to keep him in bed, or at least make him rest, and if you take my advice you'll persuade him to take you on a long honeymoon, away from work and nowhere near Brazil and his beloved Indians. If he didn't keep going back there this would have cleared up long ago.'

'I'll see what I can do,' Rebecca said with a weak smile.

'A newly married man, he'll take no persuading; you're a very lovely young woman, and he'd be a fool to refuse.' He was still chuckling as she showed him out.

Returning to the study, she rang the hotel in Brighton where Daniel was staying with his new-found relations. With a few brief words she explained the situation to Gerard Montaine, and he seemed singularly unalarmed. After a short chat to Daniel, who was thoroughly enjoying himself with his new cousins, and was at that minute waiting to leave for a picnic on the beach, she replaced the receiver and hurried back upstairs.

Benedict seemed to be in a fretful kind of sleep. Rebecca watched him for a moment, and then quickly moved around the room, gathering clean underwear from a drawer, and a simple cool blue cotton summer dress from the wardrobe. Then she headed for the shower.

She did not dare linger, and within five minutes she was back at Benedict's bedside, where she remained through the long, hot hours of the fine summer day. At two o'clock she managed to get him to take his medicine and, with a great deal of effort and not a little embarrassment, she bathed his naked, burning body and changed the sodden bedclothes.

Benedict swung between bouts of fever and sudden chills. His incoherent ramblings frequently interspersed with her name. She clung to his large hand, willing him to get better, while her own emotions fluctuated between happiness at her newfound love for him, and deep despair as to what the future might hold for her.

At one point she forced herself to go down to the kitchen, where she ate some of the cold cuts from the refrigerator without tasting anything, drank a cup of coffee and filled a jug with some orange juice for her patient, before returning to the sickroom.

The sun was setting in a glorious golden-red ball of fire, filling the room with a rose-pink haze, and Benedict was sitting up in bed, his hair ruffled, his golden eyes wild. 'Where have you been?' he demanded harshly, the evening light accentuating the planes and hollows of a face weakened by fever. 'I thought you'd left me.'

'Oh, Benedict,' she cried, rushing across to the bed; she placed the jug on the side-table, and unthinkingly grasped his hand. 'I wouldn't dream of leaving you alone. I just needed a drink.' She was sitting on the bed, cradling his large hand in hers without realising what she was giving away. 'How do you feel? I was so worried.' With her other hand she stroked the dark stubble on his unshaven jaw.

'Rebecca . . . God! I thought . . .'

For a second she was stunned by the naked vulnerability she read in his eyes, but before he could say any more she nervously interrupted. 'No, no talking, you must conserve your energy, and anyway it's time for your medicine. You must have a drink. Relax,' she said softly.

Benedict's lips twisted in a semblance of a mocking smile. 'My own Florence Nightingale.'

Hiding her face from him, she poured some juice into a glass. She loved him, but now he was coming to his senses she dared not let him see . . . Composing her features, she turned and held out the glass. 'Drink this. And here's your tablet.' In her other hand she held out the pill, but to her dismay Benedict had not the strength to hold the glass; his large hand shook and instantly she covered his hand with her own, guiding both juice and pill to his dry, cracked lips.

His head fell back against the pillows. 'Thank...' He sighed deeply, his eyes closed, and as she watched he slipped once more into a troubled sleep.

Rebecca jerked her head up. She was propped uncomfortably on the side of the bed, the deep, even tone of Benedict's breathing the only sound in the dark room. Carefully she reached out and switched on the table lamp. It was one o'clock in the morning and she was freezing. She looked with loving, tender eyes at the man lying in the bed. His fever appeared to have broken and his features were relaxed in what looked like a normal but deep sleep. She shivered, her summer dress no protection against the night air.

Benedict rolled over, muttering something in his sleep. She eyed the narrow strip of empty bed longingly. Surely if she was very careful she could wriggle under the bedclothes without disturbing him. Quickly she slipped off her dress and shoes and cautiously slid under the covers. With a weary sigh she closed her eyes. She'd rest, just a little while, she told herself. Benedict seemed over the worst, he was no longer burning up, and she was so tired...

Rebecca was cosily curled up, her cheek resting against the firm warmth of a very masculine chest. She was floating in a dream between waking and sleep. A long finger teasingly outlined her full lips. Benedict! She sighed and drew the tantalising digit into the moist, hungry heat of her mouth.

Benedict? Her eyes flew open, she pushed the hand away and, fighting the tangle of sheets, she tried to pull herself up to a sitting position.

There was a low chuckle from the man beside her, and an arm with a surprising amount of strength for a man who was ill kept her pinned to his side.

'Good afternoon, Rebecca.'

'Afternoon?' Some nurse she had turned out to be.

'One-thirty. Friday.' Benedict was leaning on one arm, staring down at her, his dark eyes tired but clear, only the gauntness of his features and the dark beard outlining his square jaw betraying the fever of the past thirty-odd hours. 'I'm back to reality, thanks to you.'

'Your medicine!' she cried.

'It can wait, but you and I can't,' he stated hardily, his hand tightening round her waist.

'But the doctor said...'

'I know what he said.'

'How could you? You were out cold when he was here yesterday.' Her eyes, wide with puzzlement, stared up into guarded dark ones. He wasn't making sense, perhaps the fever still lingered...

'Was I?' he said in a dry voice. 'A man is at his most vulnerable when ill. True, I was in the grip of a fever, but at that point I was lucid enough to hear what was being said. Maybe I refused to open my eyes because I couldn't bear the thought of seeing you refuse to look after me. I seem to remember asking you earlier to stay with me...'

'You were rambling, you didn't know what you were saying,' she excused him, stunned and not quite believing his admission of deceit.

'You're so generous, you shame me, Rebecca.' His eyes darkened as if with pain.

'Benedict.' She placed her hand on his broad chest in a gesture of comfort, and suddenly the feel of his warm flesh beneath her fingers made her aware of the intimacy of their position. 'I'd better...'

'No, Rebecca, let me talk.' His hand moved to cup her chin so she was forced to look up into his dark, intense face. 'I woke up a couple of hours ago to find your slender arm around my waist. You were curled up against my back like a soft little kitten. For a moment I thought I had died and gone to heaven.'

She felt the colour creeping under her skin at the heated glow she saw in his eyes. Was it possible he cared about her? No, she answered her own question. 'Yes, well, you're still alive,' she replied, deliberately prosaic.

But Benedict ignored her and continued. 'Then reality struck. I have lain here for ages, watching you sleep, planning what I was going to say to you.'

'There's no need to explain...' The idea of him watching her sleep was oddly disturbing.

'Rebecca, I might never have the courage again.' His sensuous lips twisted in a wry smile 'Or perhaps be weak enough again, so please listen. I love you. I always have and I always will...'

CHAPTER NINE

IT WAS the last thing in the world Rebecca had expected. She was struck dumb, her mouth fell open, and her pulse-rate shot up like a rocket. In the lengthening silence she could sense the increasing tension in the air, but was incapable of response. She couldn't believe it... but oh, how she wanted to! And deep inside her she felt the first flicker of hope.

'Rebecca!' Benedict stared at her with a pleading hunger she had never seen before. 'I'm not asking you to love me. I don't deserve you, I know, but I...I thought...' For such a proud man, he was unusually hesitant. 'I know I said I would let you and Daniel go to the country together, but...well, maybe we could come to a more amicable arrangement... The other night I was a brute, but I swear it won't ever happen again... We could have a good marriage——' He stopped and, totally out of character, his gaunt face flushed with embarrassment, but a grim determination lit his golden-brown eyes. 'I thought, I hoped, because you have looked after me, changed me, bathed me—— I can't believe you would do that if you really hated me——'

'Benedict,' she interrupted cautiously, 'you're the one who hated *me*, for hiding Daniel from you. You said as much last night...'

'Are you mad?' he asked with an edge of anger. 'Whatever you thought you heard in my ramblings, it certainly wasn't that. I tried to tell you about Gordon. I seem to remember demanding you understand, and you said yes.'

'I was humouring you. You were delirious.'

'Hell's teeth, Rebecca, you are, without a doubt, the most infuriating, stubborn, obtuse woman I have ever met.'

This was the Benedict she knew and loved, she thought wonderingly, as he moved over her, supporting himself on his elbows each side of her body. She was intensely aware of his lower torso lying over her bare legs, her briefs the only barrier between herself and his naked body. 'I think you're still delirious,' she muttered quietly, but he heard her.

'Damn it, woman, I am not delirious! I'm trying to explain. Something I tried five years ago, and again last week in France, and again last night. But this time I am not letting you out of this bed until you *listen* and *understand*. Is that clear?' he snarled.

'Yes, Benedict,' she said meekly. God knew, there was so much confusion, so much hurt between them! It was way past time they tried to talk like civilised human beings, she thought, and there was Daniel to consider. For his sake alone she owed it to Benedict to hear him out.

'First I have to know, did you believe me last week when I explained about writing to you?'

'Yes, of course, and even if I hadn't, your uncle Gerard explained what had happened at the wedding reception. In fact he apologised; he seemed to think it was partly his fault you had believed what you did about Gordon's death.'

'Thank God for Gerard!' Benedict said bluntly. 'But I have a confession to make. I didn't tell you the whole truth in the letter.'

Warily she searched his sombre face, not sure she wanted to hear any more.

'I'd better start at the beginning, Rebecca. From the moment I saw you sitting in the front row of the lecture theatre...' he breathed deeply '... I was bowled over. A tiny, exquisitely proportioned girl with the face of an angel, huge pansy eyes sparkling with life, the most intelligent expressive features...everything about you fascinated me, and then I saw Rupert. I knew you weren't his wife, and immediately jumped to the wrong conclusion. Later, at the party, I couldn't look at you when you were introduced. I didn't dare, I was afraid of making a fool of myself. No woman had ever reached me so deeply before. Later I couldn't help myself when Rupert insisted on introducing you again. But when he said your full name I couldn't believe fate could play such a trick. The girl I had wanted on sight had belonged to my half-brother.'

Rebecca felt the flame of hope in her heart burn brighter as she listened to Benedict's deep voice. It was as if he was talking to himself.

'My mother had told me about Gordon's death—her version—and, as you know, foolishly I believed her, even though Gerard, without going into details, had already told me it was an accident. In any case Gordon had been dead four years, there was nothing I could do. But when I realised who you were I felt guilty as hell. I was lusting after my dead brother's lover. I was so mixed up; maybe you were the temptress my mother had said you were. I used Gordon as a defence, to fight my own feelings... I was obsessed by you. I wanted to possess you body and soul. I tried to stay away from you, but I couldn't. Suddenly it made sense that you had ensnared Gordon, because one look at you and *I* was completely enslaved.'

Rebecca looked up at him. The intensity of his words, the sincerity in his dark eyes, was very convincing; and hadn't it been the same for her? She had loved him on sight; was it so difficult to believe Benedict had done the same?

'I can't see you as anyone's slave,' she murmured
softly, her gaze falling to his wide shoulders, the rhythmic
movement of his broad chest only a hand span away.
Unconsciously she reached out one finger, teasing a lock
of softly curling body hair, a warmth building up inside
her.

'I couldn't either at the time, though I seem to remember telling you on our wedding night I was your
willing slave.' He caught her teasing finger and kissed
it.

He had, but Rebecca had ignored his remark at the
time, too full of her own anger and resentment. Dared
she begin to believe he cared? She was still not convinced, and her doubt showed in the guarded look she
gave him.

'I don't blame you for doubting me, Rebecca. But
hear me out. I fought, God, how I fought against the
emotions you aroused in me. I told myself the years in
the jungle must have addled my brain. I didn't believe
in love, never had and never would, but one glance from
your sparkling eyes and my mind turned to mush. I lied
to myself. As long as I could believe I was seeking vengeance for my brother, I had an excuse, and didn't have
to admit that deep down I felt I was betraying him,
lusting after his woman... The night I made love to you
here in this bed——' his eyes darkened, and his head
lowered, brushing a light kiss across her brow, as though
he needed the contact '—it was the most wonderful and
the most shattering experience of my life. To discover
you were a virgin, had never belonged to Gordon, or
any other man, left me so stunned, so confused, I didn't
know what to think. I'll never forgive myself for the way
I lashed out at you. The things I said about you and
Gordon were just to cover my own guilty passion.'

'But you never intended the engagement or to marry me?' He might have lusted after her, but it still hurt, even now, to know he had not loved her.

'Yes, I did, Rebecca, I just hadn't admitted it to myself; but I spent the rest of that night awake and going over everything that had happened between us. I think I knew subconsciously even then that you weren't capable of what I had accused you of, and I knew without a doubt that I didn't want our relationship to end. Suddenly being engaged to you was vitally important to me, and marriage...yes, why not? I, who had never believed in the institution! In my conceit I thought all I had to do was telephone you in the morning and we would be back together. But I was too late, and too proud to beg.'

He had called, and he had suggested they carry on as before. Rebecca thought back. But only in a very casual way. Then she remembered something else that had always puzzled her. 'You said I looked upset on the train, but you never got out of the car at the station.'

'You didn't look back, Rebecca. If you had, you would have seen me running along the platform after you. I watched you sit in the window-seat with your head bent and tears in your lovely eyes, and cursed myself for fifty kinds of fool.'

She wanted to believe him—maybe if he had said something at the time, she would have done—but the years between had taught her caution if nothing else. 'You could have said something later at the christening,' she said quietly, a question in her voice.

'I intended to, but you were so cool, so composed. I was intimidated.'

'Now that I cannot believe.' She smiled up into his serious face. 'Five-foot-nothing scaring you...?'

'Rebecca, one frosty glance from your expressive eyes is enough to make me quake in my shoes. Haven't you realised that yet?'

She searched his handsome face with those same eyes and could see no trace of mockery; instead he looked grim.

'Then Mary made me so angry, suggesting I had seduced you. I was furious to think that you had discussed our lovemaking with her. I completely lost my temper with you.'

She remembered their fight in the study. He wasn't the only one who had lost his temper. She had made some very hurtful comments herself.

'I tried to tell you last night... No, the night before,' he corrected. 'You were right at the christening when you tore into me and told me I was trying to put my own feeling of guilt on to you, but it took me a long time to realise it.' For a moment there was silence as Benedict appeared to search for words, a distant look in his golden eyes.

'We were never a close family and I certainly felt no guilt when I took a two-year sabbatical from the family firm. My mother was quite content with my stepfather, who incidentally had been my father's right-hand man, and ran the business as well if not better than my dad had. Also young Gordon was earmarked for the business world, plus my uncle's son Jean-Paul; my presence wasn't essential. But with hindsight I can see, when I returned four years later and found out about the death of my stepfather and Gordon, I did feel guilty. I never seemed to be there when my mother needed me. Which is why I was inclined to believe her about Gordon's death. I felt as though I owed her my support, I'd been there so rarely for her.'

The pain in his eyes touched Rebecca's heart. She could understand his reasoning, even though she had been the

person hurt by it. 'I should never have accused you of
not caring for your family; you couldn't help being away
for so long.' She tried to console him. 'I had no right,
but I was so furious—hurt and furious,' she finally admitted, while her hand unconsciously stroked gently over
his chest, the heat of his body against hers. The content
of his words was inducing a melting warmth within her.
She let her other hand trace the hair arrowing down his
stomach, and she felt him flinch.

'Don't do that,' he rasped, his voice suddenly hoarse.
'I want to clear the air between us ... first.'

Flushing, she clasped her hands in front of her breasts.
She hadn't realised what she was doing, but his hard,
muscular thighs straddling her legs made her squirm
restlessly, and Benedict groaned.

'For God's sake, keep still! Or are you trying to
torment me?' His eyes clashed with hers, and for a
moment the naked longing she saw in the golden depths
stunned her.

'I was saying——' his mouth twisted '—I was trying
to tell you. You were correct, Rebecca, I did feel guilty,
hellishly guilty. From our first date, I knew in my heart
there was no way you could be in any way responsible
for Gordon's death. You were so honest, so open in your
feelings, but I ... I was so much older and terrified of
the way you made me feel. I'd never been in love before,
and in some crazy, mixed-up way I thought I had to
fight against it. But I wanted you ... God, how I want
you!'

He lapsed back into the present tense, much to
Rebecca's delight. She still couldn't quite believe his
earlier avowal of love, but gradually she was beginning
to accept that at the very least he cared something for
her.

'You have to understand, Rebecca, I felt as though I
was lusting after my brother's lover. Oh, I know Gordon

was dead, but he had loved you. Every time I held you, kissed you, ached for you, it was with a passion riddled with guilt.' He grimaced. 'I was so angry with myself, and I took it out on you.'

'You had no need,' she said softly.

'I know that now, but at the time I felt as if I was betraying Gordon. When I finally began to think rationally, and realised there was no reason to feel guilty, it was too late and I had lost you.'

Of course, in his delirium he had said she was right, and mentioned a 'guilty passion'. Now she understood. But could she believe him? Rebecca glanced up at him; letting her hands slide up to his broad shoulders, she searched his face. His handsome features were dark with a two-day stubble which gave him a piratical air, but the vulnerability in his shadowed eyes touched her heart.

'Can you ever forgive me, trust me again, as you did when we first met, before I threw it all away?' he asked.

She stroked one hand around the back of his neck, a warm tide of love sweeping through her, breaking down all the barriers of hurt and pride she had built up over the years. 'I can forgive you.' A glittering light flared in his eyes. 'But can you forgive me?' she asked softly. 'I quite deliberately deprived you of our son. When he was born I was so furious that I was alone, so passionately telling myself I hated you, I didn't even name you as his father. I had no right to do that, not to Daniel and not to you. I've spent the last four years feeling guilty——'

'It doesn't matter, Rebecca,' he cut in, and planted an affectionate kiss on her nose. 'When I found out about Daniel, I was furious with you for keeping him from me, but deep down inside I was delirious with joy.'

She sighed as his warm breath caressed her face. 'Because you had a son...'

'That, yes... but also because it meant at last I could make you marry me...'

'But if it hadn't been for Daniel, I would never have seen you again,' she said sombrely, knowing it was true.

Benedict moved, one arm locking around her waist; he rolled over on to his side, and held her imprisoned in the curve of his arm, with his free hand he stroked the tumbled curls from her brow. His dark eyes bored down into hers.

'How can you believe that, Rebecca? When I saw you again last week in France, I thought at long last the gods were smiling on me. I watched you on the beach with the children, and you were exactly as I had imagined you for years. I told myself that surely, after all this time, you would forgive me for my abominable behaviour, and give me a second chance.

'The two days we spent with the children gave me some hope, but you were wary. I didn't blame you for that, but you seemed willing to accept my friendship, and then when we went out to dinner and I realised you had never received my letter, but you still listened and appeared to believe me, I was euphoric. I was convinced I could win you back. I would have married you, Daniel or no Daniel, never doubt it,' he said fiercely, adding with a grim smile, 'have you forgotten the way I jumped on you like a sex-starved fool that night on the beach?

'No.' She would never forget; she had been seconds away from letting him take her, and she trembled at the memory. Her breasts rubbed against his chest and she could feel them swell against the soft lace of her bra. Benedict flung one heavy thigh over her slender legs, trapping her tightly against him, his own aroused state very obvious.

'I had it all planned. I was going to see you the next night, get your address, and visit you in London. I thought if I wined and dined you, courted you properly,

I could make you forget the Josh bloke you bought the
cognac for.'

Rebecca felt him stiffen and could feel the tension in
him, and noted the unasked question in his dark, intent
gaze.

'Josh and Joanne are a married couple I've known
since university. They live in Corbridge in the north of
England and Daniel and I have spent most of the school
holidays with them. They have a daughter, Amy, and
when I had to take the school trip they looked after
Daniel for me. That's why I bought the cognac.' She
should have explained long ago, but her own stiff-necked
pride had stopped her.

'Oh, God, is there no end to my idiocy?' Benedict
groaned. 'At the reception, I was furious when Daniel
mentioned Josh. I dashed you back here and virtually
raped you, I was so mad with jealousy,' he said thickly.
'How can I expect you to forgive me? Once Dolores had
dropped her bombshell about a child, I stampeded you
into marriage simply because it was too good a chance
to miss.'

'You implied I had received your letter and deliberately ignored it, to spite you. It hurt to think you had
such a low opinion of me.' That still rankled.

His lips twisted in a wry, self-mocking smile. 'I was
so furiously angry; I'd spent two days running back and
forward to your apartment, and I was mad with jealousy.
I had nightmare visions of you spending the weekend
with Josh or some other lover, and by the time I finally
found you at home I was ready to kill you for what you
had put me through. But, once I'd met Daniel and we
had put him to bed together, all I wanted to do was crawl
into bed with his mother.'

'You could have done,' she said huskily. 'But you
turned me down.' His rejection had hurt unbearably at
the time.

'I was a fool. I wanted to prove to myself that the physical attraction between us was as strong for you as it was for me. I had the stupid idea that if I could leave you feeling frustrated you'd be all the more willing to marry me. Instead you went to bed and slept like a top, and I lay awake all night on that tiny hard sofa in a state of semi-permanent arousal.'

Rebecca chuckled. 'How do you know I slept like a top?'

'Because about four in the morning I gave up and decided to join you, only to see you sprawled across your narrow bed, deeply asleep.'

Meeting his eyes, Rebecca's lips parted in a slow, sensuous smile. 'You should have done,' she murmured throatily. Her slender arms curved around his neck. They still had a lot to sort out, a lot of adjustments to make, but she no longer doubted him, she realised, happiness bubbling inside her, and they had already wasted five years. They had a lifetime to talk...

At Rebecca's urging Benedict's dark head bent and his mouth burned along the soft line of her cheek as he whispered fiercely, 'I do love you, Rebecca; if you believe nothing else, you must believe that, and I swear if you'll give me another chance I'll spend the rest of my life trying to win your love.'

His lips moved against her skin and the vibration from his words seemed to echo right through to her heart's core. Her fingers tangled in the dark silk of his hair, holding him close. 'You won't have to try very hard.' She believed him, she had to, simply because she loved him.

Benedict jerked his head back, his piercing dark eyes intent upon her flushed face. 'You mean...?'

'Yes. I think I love you...' She breathed a deep, shaky breath; she had gone as far as she dared. Her tongue

touched his lips, and she was trembling with the forc
of her emotions.

Benedict groaned and captured her mouth; the kis
was like nothing they had ever shared before. It promise
tenderness and love, forgiveness and hope. He moved
rolling her over on top of him without taking his mout
from hers. His long fingers quickly dispensed with he
bra, and his hands slid to her buttocks and the edge o
her briefs.

She felt the shudder that rippled through his hug
frame, and a responsive tremor shivered up her spine
then sanity prevailed. Lifting her head, she stared down
at his darkly flushed face, the deepening passion re
flected in his golden-brown eyes. 'You're supposed t
be ill, Benedict, this can't be good for you.'

He slipped her briefs down, his hand lingering be
tween her legs with devastating effect. She groaned, 'B
sensible...' and it was the last word she uttered for som
considerable time.

Benedict touched his lips to the tender curve of he
neck, and lower to her breast, and then nipped lightl
with his teeth. One large hand moved up and down he
back, over her bottom, sensuously kneading the rounde
cheeks, while his other hand continued an intimate ex
ploration between her thighs. She arched instinctively
fitting her soft feminine curves over the hard masculin
frame.

'Rebecca, take me,' he rasped, his eyes holding hers
'Show me you want me...this time.' His hands frame
her face. 'Please.'

He was giving her control, and with a flash of insigh
she realised he needed her to show him she wanted him
Every other time they had made love on his insistence
A slow, sexy smile curved her full lips, as she sat up
her legs straddling him, taking his hard shaft deep insid
her. She savoured the complete, full feeling, then slowl

she moved, loving the control her position gave her. He was hers, and, throwing her head back, her small hands resting on his broad chest, she moved again, her muscles contracting around him, fierce, primitive pleasure flooding through her.

Suddenly she was no longer in control. His strong hands encircled her tiny waist, urging her on and down, his mouth closed over her breast and she cried out when he withdrew the contact. He growled husky, erotic words of encouragement, his big body bucking beneath her, stroking faster and faster as the tension built until finally exploding in a mutual, fiery rapture.

His huskily rasped, 'I love you,' brought a breathless smile to her lips, as she sank down on top of him. Exhausted, she sheltered in his powerful arms, feeling protected and at peace.

The ringing of the telephone brought a reluctant groan from Benedict, and, tucking her into his side, carefully pulling the sheet up and over them at the same time, he reached out a long arm to the bedside telephone. 'Yes? Benedict Maxwell speaking.'

Curled up against him, Rebecca listened to the one-sided conversation. It was his uncle, calling to enquire about his health.

'Let me speak to Daniel,' she murmured.

'Wait your turn, woman,' Benedict said, with a grin. She listened, a smile on her face as he talked to their son, the love and pride in his tone obvious. She let her hand roam down over his flat, hard stomach to his thighs, her fingers teasing him deliberately until, with a muffled groan, he muttered, 'You win, your turn,' and handed her the phone.

Her conversation was brief as Benedict returned her teasing, his large hands caressing with unmistakable intent. Assured Daniel was fine, she hastily handed the instrument back to Benedict, his uncle once more on the line. Reluctantly reminding herself that Benedict had been ill, she moved to the far side of the bed.

He shot her a puzzled glance then returned to his conversation.

It was obviously business, but suddenly Rebecca stiffened at the mention of Fiona Grieves. She had forgotten all about the woman in the euphoria of her husband's arms.

'Yes, fine. OK.' Benedict replaced the receiver and, turning, reached for her. 'Now where were we?' he growled throatily.

'Fiona Grieves,' she said flatly, holding him at arm's length with one small hand.

'What about her?' he queried with a puzzled grin.

'How come she's working for you?'

'You're not jealous, are you, Rebecca, of me and Fiona?' A grin of pure male satisfaction creased his handsome face.

'No,' she muttered untruthfully, flushing scarlet.

He threw his head back and laughed out loud. 'You're a terrible liar, Rebecca, your blush gives you away.'

'I'm getting up,' she said huffily.

Instantly serious, Benedict reached out and hauled her back into his arms. 'Fiona means nothing to me. Three years ago she came to me and asked if I could get her a job out of the country. She was in a bit of a state; after spending ten years as Chancellor Foster's mistress, she had finally realised it was hopeless. He had no intention of ever leaving his wife for her.'

Rebecca's eyes widened in shock and disbelief. 'You mean she was having an affair with him?' she exclaimed. But, looking back down the years, she realised it could be true. The woman was always at Foster's side.

Benedict pressed a soft kiss to her head. 'Rebecca, you must have been one of the few people in Oxford not to know about it. Anyway, I felt sorry for her, and, my suspicious darling...' he held her close, his hand rubbing gently up and down her back in comfort and reassurance '...that's all I have ever felt for her. I arranged with Uncle Gerard for Fiona to work in the Bordeaux office, and she does her work very well, by all accounts.'

'Oh,' Rebecca mumbled inanely.

'Haven't you realised yet how very much I love you? I won't allow anything or anyone to come between us ever again, Rebecca.'

As his arms tightened around her she wound hers firmly around his neck, love and happiness lighting her violet eyes, curling her full lips into a blazing smile of such beauty, Benedict caught his breath, before capturing her lips with his own.

Later they showered, a very long shower, and it was midnight before they made it downstairs to the kitchen for a makeshift meal of sandwiches, crisps and champagne, then returned to bed.

The sound in her ears had to be a drum, Rebecca thought in confusion, her eyes flying open. She sat up in bed, and a large hand reached in front of her, tucking the sheet around her naked breasts.

'For my eyes only.' A soft chuckle accompanied the whispered words. She flushed scarlet and shot a sidelong glance at Benedict; his muscular upper torso was propped against the headboard and he was laughing.

'Mummy, Daddy, look what Uncle gave me.' And a live torpedo shot across the room, a small drum on a rope around his neck, his little arms swirling the drumsticks like a demented dervish.

'I'm sorry about this. His uncle brought him back an hour ago, and I've tried to keep him amused, but he refuses to wait any longer to see you both.' Mrs James's apologetic voice battled against the unholy row, as Daniel stood at the bedside, banging away incessantly.

'Your uncle must really hate you, Benedict,' Rebecca murmured drily, casting a baleful eye from the drum to his handsome face.

'Who cares, when I have your love?' he said confidently. His sensual, reminiscent smile told her exactly what he was remembering, and she grinned.

Daniel stopped drumming. 'And mine, Daddy.'

Benedict leant forward and swung Daniel, drum and all, up in his arms, hugging him to his chest.

Rebecca swallowed hard at the moisture in her husband's eyes, her last doubt gone. He was going to be a wonderful father.

'Do Daddies and Mummies always lie in bed all morning?' Daniel asked, wriggling out of his father's hold and into the bed between the two adults, once more banging his drum.

'Obviously not with a son like you,' Benedict chuckled, wrapping his arms around both mother and son in an exuberant bear-hug.

Mrs James quietly withdrew; she'd cancel breakfast and make a brunch, she thought. She wiped the moisture from her eye with the edge of her apron. They didn't need her. They had it all...

HARLEQUIN®

Don't miss these Harlequin favorites by some of our most distin-
guished authors!
And now, you can receive a discount by ordering two or more titles!

HT#25409	THE NIGHT IN SHINING ARMOR by JoAnn Ross	$2.99	☐
HT#25471	LOVESTORM by JoAnn Ross	$2.99	☐
HP#11463	THE WEDDING by Emma Darcy	$2.89	☐
HP#11592	THE LAST GRAND PASSION by Emma Darcy	$2.99	☐
HR#03188	DOUBLY DELICIOUS by Emma Goldrick	$2.89	☐
HR#03248	SAFE IN MY HEART by Leigh Michaels	$2.89	☐
HS#70464	CHILDREN OF THE HEART by Sally Garrett	$3.25	☐
HS#70524	STRING OF MIRACLES by Sally Garrett	$3.39	☐
HS#70500	THE SILENCE OF MIDNIGHT by Karen Young	$3.39	☐
HI#22178	SCHOOL FOR SPIES by Vickie York	$2.79	☐
HI#22212	DANGEROUS VINTAGE by Laura Pender	$2.89	☐
HI#22219	TORCH JOB by Patricia Rosemoor	$2.89	☐
HAR#16459	MACKENZIE'S BABY by Anne McAllister	$3.39	☐
HAR#16466	A COWBOY FOR CHRISTMAS by Anne McAllister	$3.39	☐
HAR#16462	THE PIRATE AND HIS LADY by Margaret St. George	$3.39	☐
HAR#16477	THE LAST REAL MAN by Rebecca Flanders	$3.39	☐
HH#28704	A CORNER OF HEAVEN by Theresa Michaels	$3.99	☐
HH#28707	LIGHT ON THE MOUNTAIN by Maura Seger	$3.99	☐

Harlequin Promotional Titles

#83247	YESTERDAY COMES TOMORROW by Rebecca Flanders	$4.99	☐
#83257	MY VALENTINE 1993	$4.99	☐
	(short-story collection featuring Anne Stuart, Judith Arnold, Anne McAllister, Linda Randall Wisdom)		

(limited quantities available on certain titles)

	AMOUNT	$
DEDUCT:	**10% DISCOUNT FOR 2+ BOOKS**	$
ADD:	**POSTAGE & HANDLING**	$
	($1.00 for one book, 50¢ for each additional)	
	APPLICABLE TAXES*	$ _____
	TOTAL PAYABLE	$ _____
	(check or money order—please do not send cash)	

To order, complete this form and send it, along with a check or money order for the
total above, payable to Harlequin Books, to: **In the U.S.:** 3010 Walden Avenue,
P.O. Box 9047, Buffalo, NY 14269-9047; **In Canada:** P.O. Box 613, Fort Erie, Ontario,
L2A 5X3.

Name: _____

Address: _____ City: _____

State/Prov.: _____ Zip/Postal Code: _____

*New York residents remit applicable sales taxes.
 Canadian residents remit applicable GST and provincial taxes.

HBACK-JM

POSTCARDS FROM EUROPE

HARLEQUIN PRESENTS®

Travel across Europe in 1994 with
Harlequin Presents. Collect a new
Postcards From Europe title each month!

Don't miss
DESIGNED TO ANNOY
by Elizabeth Oldfield
Harlequin Presents #1636

*Available in March wherever
Harlequin Presents books are sold.*

HPPFE3

Hi—

*Have arrived safely in
Germany, but Diether
von Lössingen denies
that he's the baby's
father. Am determined
that he shoulder his
responsibilities!*

Love, Sophie

*P.S. Diether's shoulders
are certainly wide
enough.*

**Fifty red-blooded, white-hot, true-blue hunks
from every State in the Union!**

Look for MEN MADE IN AMERICA! Written by some of our most poplar authors, these stories feature fifty of the strongest, sexiest men, each from a different state in the union!

Two titles available every other month at your favorite retail outlet.

In March, look for:

TANGLED LIES by Anne Stuart (Hawaii)
ROGUE'S VALLEY by Kathleen Creighton (Idaho)

In May, look for:

LOVE BY PROXY by Diana Palmer (Illinois)
POSSIBLES by Lass Small (Indiana)

You won't be able to resist MEN MADE IN AMERICA!